Maggie on the Cusp

Transcendence | Book 2

Lynne Cantwell

hearth/myth

Table of Contents

Chapter 1

And here I thought being home would be restful.

I'd just spent several months straightening out my ex-husband's family issues – which included finding the son he fathered at thirteen with his older sister – and had finally gotten other relatives to step up and help my ex-mother-in-law through her convalescence after cancer surgery. The trip took much longer than I had expected at the outset, and that cost me my job with the local casino. But it was worth it in many other ways, particularly in bringing me closer to my own children.

So I felt like I was leaving behind in Maryland a job well done, at least for now. And I was looking forward to going home to Lawrenceburg, Indiana – even though I was going to have to look for work as soon as I got back. I needed to be in familiar surroundings. I yearned for life to be normal again.

But when I stopped at my mother's house the morning after I got back, she didn't recognize me. Not even when I showed her the tarnished copper turtle effigy that I've had on a chain around my neck since I was a kid. She recognized the turtle just fine, but not the woman wearing it.

"Oh! That's Margie's!" she had said, using the nickname I'd abandoned in my teens in favor of Maggie, in honor of Rod Stewart's song "Maggie May." "Come on in, and I'll tell you how she came to have it."

As I smiled and nodded to my mother's pleasant chatter, my thoughts whirled. Mom's memory had not been in such bad shape when I left. Oh, sure, she'd had her forgetful moments, but don't we all, as we age? I'd certainly had more than my usual share of brain farts in the past few years, and I was only fifty-eight. Mom had thirty years on me, but she had never not known who I was before this. True, I'd been away for some time – but I didn't think two months would be long enough for such a dramatic transformation.

Eventually, Mom wound down. We were seated in the living room — I had gravitated to my usual spot on the sofa, but Mom had insisted I take the "guest chair," which was prettier but less comfortable than the other seats in the room — and I jumped into the silence with both feet. "So where's Margie now?" I asked.

"Oh, she's helping a friend out on the East Coast," Mom said. She was not the sort to reveal her family's dirty laundry to a stranger, and so she didn't tell this new woman that Margie had been summoned to dance attendance on her controlling ex-mother-in-law.

"She's a good person for doing that," I said, hoping God overlooked my hubris in complimenting myself, given the situation. "How long has she been gone, Mrs. Muir?"

Mom paused. "Well, I don't know," she said after a moment. "It seems like it's been a long time. She was such a little thing — and standing up to me like that, with that filthy turtle held behind her back!" She chuckled.

I knew she had slipped into the memory of little Margie, and so I tried to bring her back to the present. "But Margie must be grown now," I said reasonably, "if she traveled all the way to Maryland to help her friend."

"Oh, yes, she is." Mom nodded. "She has children of her own. Three of them. I'm a great-grandma, you know."

"That's wonderful," I said. "You must be very proud of Margie."

She frowned. "That's not right."

"What's not right?"

"She's not… She doesn't call herself…" All of a sudden, she looked hard at me. "What is this, April Fool's Day? Why are you trying to trick me? Coming in here like you don't know me. My own daughter!"

"Me?" I said, laughing, though fear was still clutching at my chest. "You're the one who pretended I was a stranger."

"But you showed me the turtle at the door!"

"You locked me out!"

She looked offended. "I would never do any such thing to you."

Well, at least she recognized me. We could deal with the revisionist history later. "Okay, Mom," I said with a placating nod. "Anyway. Do you want to hear about my trip?"

"Sure," she said.

She still looked a little dazed, so I gave her the *Readers' Digest* version. "Ruth got through her surgery fine. She's starting radiation treatments this coming week, and Debbie's going to take her." Ruth Brandt was my ex-mother-in-law; Debbie was her eldest daughter.

Mom's eyes widened. "*Debbie?* But she wouldn't give her mother the time of day!"

"For good reason," I said, and explained that she'd been sent away as a teenager to have a child out of wedlock – a baby boy, fathered by my ex-husband, Gene Brandt. "Once Debbie got out from under Ruth's thumb, she had no interest in going back."

"I can't imagine why," Mom said dryly. Then, "Where are my manners? Do you want something to drink?"

"I'll get it," I said, glad for an excuse to escape the guest chair. From the kitchen, I called, "Want some water?"

"Sure," she said. "So what happened to the baby?"

"Adopted by a couple in Baton Rouge. He's a truck driver." I brought the glasses out and handed one to her.

"My stars," said Mom, as I took my accustomed spot on the couch. "What did Gene say when all this came out?"

"He wasn't thrilled." I winced, flashing back to the murderous look he had given me as we tussled over the shoebox that held Lenny's birth certificate. "He basically got in his car and drove away." I made a mental note to touch base with Riley, Gene's new wife, to make sure she was okay. "Oh, but there's good news," I went on, grinning. "I got to see Beatrice."

"You did?" she asked with a surprised smile.

"I did. And I met her husband John, and her kids, Royce and Ryker."

"How wonderful!" Mom was beaming.

"Want to see pictures?" I pulled my phone out of my jeans pocket.

"Just a minute. Let me find my reading glasses." Mom looked on the end table beside her, on the coffee table, on the TV stand. "Now where did I put those darned things?" she said, somewhat peevishly, and went off down the hall toward her bedroom. As she went, I marveled that she was still getting around so well. Ruth was younger than my mother by several years, but Mom moved more easily than Ruth did. Of course, pain might have been slowing Ruth down. But still, for eighty-eight, my mother was pretty spry.

She was gone for a long time. At first, I sipped my glass of water and busied myself with looking through the pictures I'd taken over the past few weeks, deciding which ones to show my mother. Then I played a hand or two of solitaire on the phone. Still she hadn't returned. I finally got up and went down the hall to find her. "Did you get lost?" I called out cheerfully.

She had, in a manner of speaking. My mother had evidently forgotten why she'd gone into her bedroom. Instead of looking for her reading glasses, she had put on her nightgown and gone to bed in the middle of the day.

"Mom?" I said quietly, but she didn't move. I crept around the bed until I could see her face. Her breathing was regular, her mouth slightly open. "Mom?" I said again. No response. She was fast asleep.

I stowed my phone and let myself out of the house, locking up behind me. Then I got in my car and just sat for a minute, staring at nothing.

My mother was clearly losing touch with reality.

This wasn't the sort of forgetfulness that Ruth had suffered from — the kind brought on by stressful situations. I had eventually figured out what was going on with my ex-mother-in-law, and was able to manage it somewhat and excuse the rest. But this thing with Mom was looking like full-blown dementia.

The puzzling thing was that it had come on so suddenly. Back when I was a kid, living in this house, we'd had a neighbor lady named Mrs. O'Meara who suffered from some form of dementia. She was fine, if a little forgetful, when we first moved in – but over time, she got to where she didn't remember any of us. Of course, back then we didn't call it dementia; we called it going crazy. My brother Sandy was particularly vicious behind her back, although he was always polite when he had to make conversation with her. Mrs. O'Meara was pretty easy to talk to, as long as you didn't challenge her reality, and as long as you didn't pick any of her flowers. She had a nurse – a black woman named Miss Betty – who lived in the house and took care of her.

Mrs. O'Meara died while I was in college. Her pale blue house was sold to a young couple who painted it mustard yellow with brown trim, and populated it with a couple of kids. Miss Betty presumably found herself a position with another senile old lady.

I found myself wondering whether I could locate her. Maybe we could hire her to look after Mom. After all, she knew the neighborhood.

I put my wrists on top of the steering wheel and rested my forehead on my hands. Then I let the tears flow. This was not the normal I had been looking forward to when I came home from Rockville. I allowed myself a few minutes to mourn that lost dream, that halcyon time that was never going to be. I knew I was being melodramatic; it probably would not have been anywhere near as halcyon as I had hoped it would be. But I wasn't in the mood to be realistic right then. The point was that it was gone. And what I had just witnessed – Mom going off to look for her reading glasses and going to bed instead – was going to be my new normal.

This first round of grief didn't last very long; I wasn't inclined to give my mother's neighbors any more gossip fodder than necessary. After a few minutes, I wiped my eyes, started the engine, and drove home.

Inside my apartment, I stared for a moment at the refrigerator that needed restocking and the suitcase that wasn't going to unpack itself. Then I kicked off my shoes, shucked off my jeans, and went back to bed myself.

Before I lay down, though, I took off my turtle necklace and put it in its accustomed place on the tiny table in my bedroom, between the candle and the basket of things I'd picked up on walks around the neighborhood. The turtle, at least, seemed glad to be home. For me, the jury was still out.

In a moment, it seemed, I was dreaming.

I was dozing in a pond – no, an eddy near the bank of a creek. Or maybe it was a river. It was hard to tell. In any case, I was shut up in my shell, napping in the dappled sunlight, when I heard a muffled splash and a bleat of fear. I poked my head out and opened my eyes. A doe, the white fur on her muzzle marking her as old for her people, had apparently slipped down the muddy bank and fallen into the water. She thrashed to her feet, confused. It seemed like she couldn't see the way back to shore. It occurred to me that if she just turned around, she could save herself – but she didn't seem capable of that kind of reasoning.

I stretched my legs and neck, preparing to swim to her and point her in the right direction, when a long, dark shadow glided past me. I knew in an instant what it was – Mishepeshu, the Underwater Panther. He must have either heard or sensed the doe's distress and was moving in for the kill.

I hesitated. My people lived long lives, and with long life came a perspective that might be called wisdom. Some peoples – those who lived shorter lives – believed Mishepeshu to be evil, because he took the lives of those whom they loved. But my people knew the Water Panther was not evil at all. He had his place on Turtle Island, just as I did. And if his place required him to take the life of one confused, elderly doe, at this time in the Earth's cycle of existence, then who was I to interfere?

But then the doe locked her terrified gaze with mine, and I knew several things at once. For one thing, it was not her time to die; she still had important tasks to accomplish, and cutting her life short now would cause incalculable distress later in the cycle.

For another, she and I were kin.

I cannot normally outswim a Water Panther, but I darted out to intercept him.

I had the element of surprise, but I didn't expect it to be a fair fight. He was much larger and stronger, with teeth and talons I would never possess. Still, I knocked him off-course, and we tussled for a moment as he tried to rid himself of me. At last, as he roared, I saw my chance. I swam straight for his open jaws and pulled in my extremities just as his wicked teeth came together to crush me.

But I was no ordinary turtle; I could not be crushed. He bit down hard and broke a tusk on my shell.

Screaming in pain and fury, he spat me out. I flew through the air, landing bottom-up on the bank. Now I was in a fix; I could not right myself without significant effort. The doe was at Mishepeshu's mercy, and there was nothing I could do to save her.

But Mishepeshu's roaring got softer, and I could hear the turbulent water near me calming. I had done it! The Water Panther was swimming away!

I stuck out my legs and tail, and began the arduous task of flipping myself right-side up again. But the rescued turned rescuer; a soft nose wedged itself under the edge of my shell and raised me up so that I could flip myself over on my own.

I stuck out my head and once again met the doe's eyes. "Thanks, Mom," I said.

That brought me to wakefulness in a big hurry. *Mom?*

In dreams, they say, we are every character we dream about. So in theory, I was the scared doe, the water panther, and the turtle.

But not in this case. This hadn't been a regular dream. It was much more similar in feel to a dream I'd had in Rockville. In that one, however, I had been the water panther; this time, the water panther – Mishepeshu – had been someone else. Someone evil, no matter what the turtle had believed. And moreover, I was related to *him*, too.

I sighed and rubbed sleep from my eyes. I checked the bedside clock, and realized I'd only been asleep for a few minutes. Then I realized there was another light in the room, besides the daylight coming in around the edges of my drapes. It was coming from my turtle effigy, and it scared me. I'd seen it glow once before, but that light was a golden-copper hue; this light looked dark, if that makes any sense. Black-green, like glowing verdigris.

I crossed to the table where the turtle sat and managed to light the candle with shaking fingers. Bracing myself on the corner of the bed, I dropped to a cross-legged seat on the floor before it. Then I sank my head in my hands.

I had been the turtle, and only the turtle. The confused doe had been Mom. The water panther – the evil creature that would have taken advantage of her confusion to kill her – was my brother Sandy. And I had no idea what to do next.

Chapter 2

When I raised my head sometime later, the turtle's dirty glow had gone out. I got to my feet and hobbled to the bathroom, working the kinks out of my knees and hips as I went. At fifty-eight, I wasn't as spry as I used to be.

I rinsed my face with warm water and regarded my reflection in the mirror above the sink: my hair was gray, my cheeks and forehead creased with worry lines. None of that was new. My appearance hadn't gotten any more startling over the past few months, while I sorted through my ex-husband's family's secrets and nursed his mother through cancer surgery, but it hadn't gotten any better, either.

I dried my face and hands, and tried to think through the message my turtle had been trying to send me. Over the past few months, as I'd begun to untangle my relationship with my children, the turtle's ancient patina had begun to burn or melt away. I could see copper shining through in several spots, along the edges especially. But today, it had glowed darkly, as if the verdigris was blocking its natural aura. That made some sense – most of it was still discolored. I'd had to work hard on myself to get as much of the patina off as I had.

This message, though, seemed less about working on myself and more about working on Mom. Or Sandy. Although I had put in a lot of work on others in Rockville, too; the Brandts had locked down baby Lenny's story so tightly that even though Gene and I had been married for twenty years, I'd had no inkling he existed.

I supposed I ought to call him Lee. His given name was Leonard, and while Ruth thought of him as Lenny, his adoptive parents had called him Lee.

Anyway. This train of thought was getting me nowhere. I needed to quit thinking about Ruth and her family, and deal with the crisis here.

I knew one thing for sure: I was going to have to talk to Sandy to find out what had gone on while I was in Maryland. I'd left him in charge of Mom, as he was her only other living relative.

Mom's maiden name was Shirley Denison. She'd been the youngest of five kids; one sister died in infancy, and the two boys were killed in World War II, one in Germany and the other in the Battle of Midway. That left Mom and her oldest sister, Helen. Helen had married the boy next door, Freddy McMurty, who'd had the great good luck not only to survive the war but to come home in one piece. He was happy to run both his own parents' farm and my grandparents' place after they died. And Mom was happy to escape into the arms of George Muir, an only child whose flat feet kept him out of the Army.

Anyway, Freddy died when a freight train hit his pickup truck, which had conked out at a railroad crossing. This was back before every crossing had those protective barrier arms, of course. Some troublemaker told Aunt Helen at the funeral that he saw Uncle Freddy deliberately pull into the path of the train, but she refused to believe it. In any case, she outlived him by a good fifteen years. When she died in the early 2000s, the farm was sold to a big agriculture conglomerate.

My father was gone, too, dead of a sudden stroke when my kids were in their teens. His death gave me a plausible excuse for leaving Rockville for good: Mom took Dad's death hard, and it seemed only natural that her daughter would come home to help her get through the rough patch.

And now, here I was, about to step up again.

Sandy and his wife, Diane, lived in Indianapolis. Both of them were retired, so when Ruth demanded my presence in Maryland, I figured it wouldn't be a hardship for them to keep an eye on Mom. All they had to do was buzz down to Lawrenceburg once a week or so, just to make sure she was okay and didn't need anything.

This wasn't getting me anywhere.

I unpacked my suitcase and had a lunch of canned soup and stale saltines. Then, still at the kitchen table, I bit the bullet and called my brother.

Diane answered the phone. "Muir residence," she said, in her thin, "professional" voice. I pictured her in my mind's eye: powdered and lipsticked, with a bottle-blond bouffant hairdo. Cats'-eye reading glasses on a beaded lanyard were her only concession to aging. She always put me in mind of a superintendent of a girls' dorm – haughty, and looking to catch you out. "Who's calling, please?"

"Hi, Diane, it's Maggie."

"Oh, thank goodness you're back!"

I sat up straighter. "Why?"

"Well, it's just a relief to know we won't have to go to Lawrenceburg this week. All that driving is so hard on Sandy. He's no spring chicken anymore, you know."

It was less than a hundred miles from Mom's to Sandy and Diane's. And Sandy was only five years older than me. "I'm sorry to hear that it's so difficult for him to drive an hour and a half to see his mother," I said. Then I dialed down the snark. "I'm sorry. I do appreciate you both doing this for me. I was able to get everything done that I needed to get done."

"Hmm," she said.

"Is Sandy there? I need to talk to him about Mom."

"Why?" The note of suspicion in her voice intrigued me. It almost sounded like guilt.

"She acted a little oddly when I stopped by this morning. Is he there?"

"What do you mean, odd? What did she do?"

The woman could be difficult, but she wasn't usually this bad. "Diane, would you please put Sandy on the phone?"

"He's not here," she said. "And it's *two* hours from here to Mother Muir's house."

The way Diane addressed my mother had always irritated me. Why couldn't she just call her Mom, the way Sandy and I did? "If you say it takes Sandy two hours, I guess I have to believe you. But I've clocked it. It takes me an hour and a half."

"Maybe Sandy doesn't have a lead foot like you have."

I blinked in surprise. Then I got mad. "Just have him call me," I said, and hit the button to end the call so hard that I was lucky my finger didn't punch right through the phone.

She hadn't always been so cranky. When she and Sandy first got married and they still lived nearby, Diane would invite me over sometimes – for a ladies' lunch, she called it, or a shopping trip to Cincinnati. I'd never had a sister, and it was fun for me to have an older friend to confide in. I was fifteen then, and at that age you have questions that you just don't want to ask your mother.

It didn't take long, though, before I realized that everything I confided in Diane got back to Sandy. And he had a tendency to use anything against me that he possibly could. It didn't take me long to figure out that if I wanted to avoid being teased – or worse, judged – for every little thing I did, I needed to quit telling Diane anything.

When she noticed I'd clammed up, the invitations for girls' lunches and shop-'til-you-drop outings pretty much quit coming. That hurt. But then I wondered whether the sisterly act was all Diane's idea, or whether she and Sandy had cooked it up together. And *then* I wondered why Sandy would suggest it – and I didn't like the answer my wounded, suspicious mind came up with.

At the next family get-together, I gave both of them the cold shoulder. I believe Diane's snarky attitude toward me dated from that dinner.

Mom could hardly help but notice. "Why were you so distant to Sandy and Diane?" she asked as we did the dishes together after the pair had gone home.

"They started it," I said.

"How?"

I scrubbed a pot with unnecessary force. "Everything I tell Diane gets back to Sandy."

"That's how it works when you're married. Couples don't have secrets from one another."

I side-eyed her. "Do you tell Dad everything?"

"Well." She never finished the sentence – just busied herself with drying the silverware and putting it away, which I knew meant I'd caught her in a contradiction and she didn't want to admit it. "Anyway, you need to be nice to them. Both of them."

"Mom," I protested, "you know how Sandy is. He's a jerk!"

"He's your *brother*," she said. "When Daddy and I are gone, he's all you'll have left."

I was too young at the time to understand that her comment said more about her own growing up than it did my situation. So I rolled my eyes at her.

She glowered at me. "You at least need to be civil to them. You can manage that for a few hours every week."

"Maybe," I said. And I did try to manage it. But it was hard. Nobody was telling Diane to be nice to *me*, and sometimes she got under my skin.

Anyway, it wasn't long after that Sandy got a job in Indianapolis and they moved away. Their weekly visits became monthly, and then they got even farther apart. Eventually we only got together on the big holidays: Easter, Thanksgiving, and Christmas. Occasionally, Mom and Dad would drive up to see them, but I always begged off – homework and my job at the grocery store were good excuses. Then I went away to college, and that became an excellent excuse.

And then I got pregnant, and Gene and his mother whisked me away to Rockville, and that was pretty much it. Even after I moved back to Lawrenceburg, I rarely saw them.

Even so, I'd felt no hesitation about contacting them to help out with Mom. The way I looked at it, I was doing the majority of the heavy lifting. They could take a turn. And Sandy had agreed to do it – not gracefully, but he'd said he would. Granted, I was gone a lot longer than I'd expected to be, but still – sometimes you have to step up when family is involved. But now I wondered whether I should have gone to Diane instead of Sandy to make the request.

Or maybe I should have told Ruth to forget the whole thing. Except the trip had been a good thing in the end. Ruth was recovering, Debbie had reconciled with her mother, and Bea and I were talking again. No, I was glad I had gone to Maryland. Sandy and Diane were just going to have to get over themselves.

I tossed the rest of the box of stale crackers and made out a list for the grocery store. I told myself I was going to have to stick to the list; my savings had dwindled over the past couple of months, and I didn't know how long it would be before I could find another job. Sighing, I picked up my purse and went out to my car.

An ancient VW bus was parked at the corner.

I approached it, my smile widening. It was Zed's – I was sure of it. I'd met Zed and Granny at the Great Circle Earthworks east of Columbus, Ohio, on my way to Maryland a few months before. Granny believed herself to be the reincarnation of the Shawnee Indians' creator goddess, or so Zed had said, and Granny herself told me that my services would be needed to renew the Earth. It was all kind of mind-boggling. But still and all, I was glad to see them. I needed to run my dream past somebody and get some advice on what to do about it, and Granny seemed like the perfect person to ask.

I knocked on passenger side door, and the cargo door slid back. "Hey, Maggie," said Zed with a serious look. "Come on in."

"I'm so glad you're here," I said, clambering up into the van. "I really need to talk to Granny."

"She's not here."

I straightened in surprise, nearly conking my head on the ceiling. "She's not?"

"No. And she doesn't know I'm here talking to you. Have a seat."

Slowly, I lowered myself into a chair. "What's going on? Is she all right?"

He shook his head in disgust. "She'll be fine. We were on our way down to Mississippi – she prefers working the southern states in the winter. The cold makes her bones ache, she says. Anyway, she tripped over a curb at a rest stop near Louisville."

"Is she hurt?"

"Kinda bad, yeah," he said. His forehead creased with worry. "She's got a broken hip, and the doctors say she's gotta stay there for a few weeks."

"She's pretty tough," I said, trying to sound reassuring. "I'm sure she'll be fine." I wasn't really sure, though – not at all. It seemed to me that every story I'd ever heard of an elderly woman in declining health started with a broken hip.

He could tell, I thought. "I don't know whether she's gonna make it, Maggie," he said.

"You mean you think she'll...?"

"Oh, wait." He chuckled. "No, that's not what I meant. She's not gonna die 'til after the end of this cycle." He sobered. "No, what worries me is how much this little misadventure will set her back. She might not make her thousand-and-fifty-four."

Among the odder things I'd learned, the first time I'd met Zed, was that Granny had to rescue or redeem one-thousand-fifty-four people before the next major lunar standstill in April 2025, and I was one of her people. It was all tied in with Hopewell Indian cosmogony; one-thousand-fifty-four was their sacred unit of measurement. As crazy as it sounds, Zed and Granny's story checked out with what I knew – and what I had begun to remember in flashes of insight – from my association with my turtle effigy. And yes, I know exactly how crazy *that* sounds.

"I thought you told me she was ahead of schedule," I said now. "That she was working fast, in case something happened to make her slow down later."

"Yeah, but it wasn't supposed to happen this soon!" he said. "Look. All I'm saying is that she may need to lean on you a little harder from here on out."

"I thought I wasn't supposed to start 'til the next lunar standstill."

His eyes grew wide. "Where did you get *that* idea from?"

"From you and Granny."

He shook his head. "No, no. You've already started."

"I did? When?"

"When you were in Maryland! That whole mess with your ex-husband's family." He raised his hands, palms upturned. "You didn't know?"

"No, I… I guess I thought I was in training."

"Training!" He snorted.

"Or sorting out my own stuff so that I would be…I don't know. Pure, or something. For when I started." I faltered.

"You think the Universe would make you go through hell and sort all that stuff out, and not give you credit for it?" He shook his head again. "That's not how it works."

"So…how many people have I rescued?" I asked slowly.

He grinned archly. "How many do you think?"

"Well…" I ticked them off on my fingers. "Ruth. And Debbie. And Lenny – I mean Lee."

"And Debbie's kids and their kids," he said. "They've got their grandmother and great-grandmother back, thanks to you."

"Oh! I hadn't thought of that."

"Who else?"

"Beatrice," I said instantly.

He nodded. "And her husband and kids. Nokomtha." He reached over and nudged my knee with a grin.

I felt my face grow warm. Nokomtha was the Shawnee word for grandmother. In a flash of inspiration, I had told Bea's kids to call me that.

"And Tim? And Ana?" Tim was my youngest. He'd been called away from our family reunion to tend to his injured girlfriend in Mexico City.

"Sure. And your middle daughter, too." Emily was in grad school in California. "And Debbie's sister and her wife – and their new baby."

"I guess maybe so," I said. Abby, Ruth's middle daughter, had been caught up in the family drama, too. Maybe now she could find her way to heal. "I never thought about how many people I was helping."

"You forgot a few," he said. "What about Riley?"

Riley was Gene's second wife. She had also been one of the underage girls he'd had sex with. "I'm not sure I was all that helpful to her," I said ruefully.

"She needed to know all that stuff about Gene," Zed said. "Now she knows the score, and she can decide whether to stay or leave him."

I had been wondering what Riley would do. She had been the one to pursue Gene after our divorce, and she had been good for him. But I wasn't sure whether he had been good for *her*. If I'd been in her position, and been handed the information about Lenny's parentage, I would have left him. I mean, I *had* left him, but I would have left a lot quicker if I'd known the whole sordid story. And I wouldn't have left the kids behind.

"And Gene, too," Zed said.

"What?"

"Gene's in your column."

"I *saved* him?" I laughed humorlessly. "That's a heck of a note."

"It sounds crazy, I know," he said, "but that's how it works. What you did was to put him on the path. Now, if he falls off it, don't feel like you failed. He needs to walk the rest of the way on his own, just as we all do."

I nodded. Then I sighed. "I do wish Granny was here. I have a lot of questions for her about what's going on with my mother."

"I know," he said. "She and I talked about it a little bit before she got hurt. It's a bad situation, Maggie. I'm real sorry about that." He gazed at me with compassion.

"Do you have any advice?" I asked. "Any hints, maybe?"

He looked as if he were weighing how much he should say. At last, he said, "I can tell you this much: there's something ugly going on with your brother and his wife, and you're going to have to figure out what it is."

"Do you know what it is?" I asked.

"Nope. And I wouldn't tell you if I did."

I nodded. "I thought that's what you'd say. Rules of the game, right?"

"It's not a game," he said. "But yeah. Basically, I can't give away anything you haven't already figured out."

I nodded. My thoughts were whirling, but one thing stood out. "One more question."

"Shoot."

"Will my mom recover?"

He regarded me sadly. "Not for long."

Tears pricked the backs of my eyelids. He was right, though – I'd already figured it out. "Okay." I stood as best I could in the cramped confines of the van. "Well, I should let you get going."

"Maggie," Zed said, following me out. I turned back to him, and he put a hand on my shoulder. "You don't need to do this alone. You have people in your life who will help you, if you ask them."

I nodded. "You mean Bea."

"And Abby." He smiled at my expression. "Don't look so surprised. Diane's not your only sister, y'know."

"You're right. And Abby's been a better sister to me than Diane ever was." I smiled. "Thanks, Zed. I'm really glad you stopped by. Is there anything I can do for you and Granny?"

"Nah," he said. "Thanks for asking, but we're gonna be just fine. Granny just needs to get up out of that hospital bed so we can hit the road again." He patted my shoulder and got back in the van. Then he rolled down the driver's side window and waved. "See ya later, Maggie. You'd better get moving if you're going to the store. It looks like it's gonna snow."

I looked up at the sky in surprise. When I'd gotten in the van, it had been sunny; now it was overcast and the breeze had picked up. "Wow –

the weather changed in a hurry," I said, realizing belatedly that I was talking to no one. The van was gone. I hadn't even heard Zed start the engine.

"People come and go so quickly here," I muttered as I got in my own car.

Chapter 3

Snow was already coming down at a pretty good clip when I got to the grocery store. And the place was jammed. Apparently everyone in town had known about the snowstorm coming in but me; the checkout lines were longer than usual and some of the shelves were bare.

"Looks like they're keeping you busy," I said to Marty, who was making a valiant effort to keep the shelves of milk stocked.

"Oh, hi, Maggie," he said. Marty was a fixture around the place; I'd worked with him here when I was in high school, and again after I'd left Gene. He was what they call developmentally disabled nowadays, but he was a sweet guy – and a better worker than some who came into this world with all their faculties. "You need any milk?"

I helped myself to a couple of half gallons – one for me and one for Mom. "How much snow are we supposed to get, anyway?"

He lifted his uniform ball cap and scratched at his forehead for a moment. Then he settled his cap and said, "Five or six inches, the weatherman said. We might have a white Christmas. Can you beat that?"

"Six inches?" I said. "We never get that much this early in the season."

"That's what they're saying," he said. "You better get some bread, too, Maggie. And eggs."

"I'll do that. Why do people always stock up on that stuff when a snowstorm's coming?" I asked with a grin. "They do it in Maryland, too."

"They do?" He seemed genuinely surprised. "I couldn't say why they do it there. But my mom always makes French toast when it snows. So that's why I always bring *her* bread, milk, and eggs."

"Good thinking," I said. "I'll pick up some for my mom, too."

"Ask her to make you French toast," he called as I walked away. "It's the best thing for a snowy day. And hot chocolate, too!"

"I'll add it to the list!" I said, and hurried to finish my shopping.

The storm made for an early dusk. I thought I'd better stop at Mom's house before I went home. If the snow was going to be as bad as Marty had heard, it would be a day or two before I could get over to Mom's again. I'd heard of places where snowplows hit the streets while the snow was still falling, and people resumed their lives as soon as they shoveled themselves out. Southern Indiana, however, was not one of those places.

I had to park at the curb. A black SUV sat in the spot in Mom's driveway where I usually parked. "Now who could that be?" I muttered – and then it hit me. That was Sandy's car.

Under my coat, my turtle began to vibrate on its chain.

It was just as well, I told myself; I needed to talk to him anyway. But still I put off getting out of the car.

I know a lot of people are rotten to their siblings when they're all kids, but as they mature, they grow closer. Well, Sandy never grew out of it. I was always the dumb kid sister. His greatest joy, when we were kids, was to tease me until I cried; among his greatest joys as an adult was to find something to needle me about until I exploded. When I was a teenager, it was my hair or my weight; then, later, it was my marriage. "Why did you marry a guy named Eugene?" he would ask, laughing derisively. "What a stupid name. And he's such a poser. For God's sake, Maggie, couldn't you find somebody normal to screw around with? And what the hell were you thinking, letting him knock you up? Don't you know *anything?*"

Given Sandy's opinion of my husband – which, it galled me to admit later, wasn't far wrong – but anyway, you would think my brother would have been thrilled to learn that I was divorcing Gene. But no, that was my fault, too. "So you're just gonna give up? Marriage is supposed to be 'til death do you part, Maggie. Did you miss that part when you said your vows? Or maybe Jews don't believe in that sort of thing. Is that it?"

I'd grown up enough by then that I refused to let him see me cry when his barbs sunk to the bone. I would sit there and take it, poker-faced, with my nails digging into my palms, until eventually he would give up and go away. But I internalized the abuse. His comments became the nagging soundtrack in my head – the voice that told me it wasn't worth going back to finish college, that I might as well work at the casino with the other high school graduates who'd never made it out of our little town, because after all the things I'd screwed up in my life, that was all I deserved.

Abuse doesn't always leave a visible mark.

Sitting here only delayed the inevitable. I sucked in a breath, stiffened my spine, and got out to trudge up the snowy sidewalk with the bag of groceries for Mom. My turtle bounced in time to each step I took.

As I entered the house, I heard voices coming from the kitchen. Our house was your typical ranch-style: a long, one-story rectangle. The front door opened into the living room; the eat-in kitchen was to the immediate right, with the laundry room and entrance to the garage past that; all three bedrooms, plus the bathroom, were down the hall to the left.

"Hi, Mom," I called as I shed my coat and kicked off my boots by the front door. "I heard we were in for quite a bit of snow, so I picked up some groceries for you." As I entered the kitchen, I said, "Oh, hi, Sandy. I didn't expect to see you here."

Mom sat at the table with some official-looking papers in front of her. Sandy was hovering over her, one hand on the table and the other on the back of her chair. He looked terrible: his skin was sallow and his eyes seemed to have retracted in their sockets.

The two of them looked at me like they'd been caught with their hands in the cookie jar. "Just put those things away," Mom said, in a brusque voice that I was pretty sure was a smokescreen to cover her confusion.

"Why wouldn't I be here?" my brother challenged, straightening, and wincing as he did so. He'd wrenched his back at work a few years before, and had gone out on disability when it became too painful for him to do his job.

I shrugged. "Feel free to come whenever you want." As I put away the groceries, I gestured toward the paperwork. "What's that all about?"

"Nothing that concerns you," he said, and flipped the papers over. "Mainly I came over here to bring Mom her medication. She left it at our house when she visited with us last week. Isn't that right, Mom?"

"Sure," Mom said.

"You had a good time at our place, didn't you?"

"Sure."

"What did you guys do?" I put in. "Anything fun?"

Mom turned a blank look on me. "I don't know," she confessed.

"Aw, Mom, of course you do," he said. "We went to that new, fancy burger place. Remember? And we drove around and looked at houses."

"Sure," Mom said again.

I picked up a pill bottle on the kitchen table and read the label. It had Mom's name on it – Shirley Muir – but the prescription had been written by a doctor whose name I didn't recognize, and filled at a drugstore in Indianapolis. I looked at Sandy. "Who's Dr. Grayson?"

"Diane's doctor," he said evenly.

"Why did you take Mom to see Diane's doctor? Did something happen while I was gone?"

"Not exactly."

I wasn't in the mood for evasiveness. "Sandy, what happened to make her so confused? She wasn't like this when I left."

"Well, that's just it," he sneered. "You left. And you left us holding the bag."

"What?"

"Mom needs better care than she's getting here in East Buttfuck, Indiana. She's getting on in years, and she ought to be seeing somebody who specializes in geriatrics. Who knows what horrible condition she might have that her doctor here won't be smart enough to catch?"

I thought of Dr. Malik, Mom's general practitioner. He was a Pakistani man whom the city had recruited because so many of our old doctors had retired. It seemed no self-respecting American med school student wanted to be a G.P. in East Buttfuck, Indiana, as my brother had so charmingly put it. Dr. Malik was at least as knowledgeable as my son-in-law, John Simms in Baltimore, and maybe a little more on the ball. For one thing, I doubt he would have let Ruth get away with not taking her heart medication.

"What did Dr. Grayson say about her confusion? Yesterday, she got up while we were talking, and went in to take a nap. What's that all about, Sandy?"

"How the hell should I know? I'm not a doctor!"

"Well, things were apparently bad enough that you thought she needed to see some whiz-bang physician in Indianapolis."

"Her health is failing!" he yelled.

But she was fine when I left! I glanced at Mom. Her eyes were unfocused and her mouth was turned down at the corners. I lowered my voice to just above a hiss. "Maybe we shouldn't be talking about her as if she isn't here," I told him.

With a start, he glanced at her. Then he pointed a thumb toward the living room and led the way. I sighed heavily and followed him.

"Have a seat," he said.

"No, thanks. I'm fine right here."

"Suit yourself." He assumed a tough-guy stance, arms crossed and feet apart. "Now. I see you've finally noticed that our mother is a sick old lady. I didn't want to say this in front of her, but it was irresponsible of you to take off and leave her here all alone."

"I didn't leave her alone," I said, doing my best to keep my voice down. "You and Diane were supposed to check in on her."

"Which we did," he said, "and it was our judgment that she shouldn't be living alone at all. So we took her to our house."

"For the whole two months?"

"Well, no. For a couple of weeks."

"And then you brought her back here to be on her own again. Because she was here by herself when I came over earlier. And when I talked to Diane this morning, she seemed relieved you wouldn't have to make the trip today." I crossed my own arms. "Something's not adding up here, Sandy."

He paused for a moment. "You talked to Diane?"

"I just said so, didn't I?"

"What did she say?"

"Ask her yourself. You're the one who's married to her." Then something else occurred to me. "Wait. Mom was supposed to see Dr. Malik while I was gone. Did she go?"

"No," he said. "I just told you, she saw Dr. Grayson."

"She saw Diane's doctor instead."

"That's right."

"Why?"

He looked at me as if I'd grown a second head. "I can't believe I have to spell it out for you," he said. "He's a Moozlum."

"He's a what?" Then I did the translation in my head, and stared at him in dismay. "Oh, no. Don't tell me you're one of *those* idiots."

His expression closed like a fist. "I won't have my mother treated by some foreign doc who wants us all to live under sharia law!"

"You haven't even met the guy!" I said. "He was born in Michigan, for God's sake!"

"Keep your voice down," he growled.

"Not a chance," I said. "And I won't let you take over Mom's care, either. I don't know what you're up to, Sandy, but it's not going to work."

"You're crazy!" he said. "Both of you are crazy! You're paranoid or something, and she's – she's – " He shook a finger toward the kitchen.

"Get out," I said. I felt my turtle warming under my shirt.

His upraised hand closed into a fist. "You're kicking me out of our childhood home?"

"I'm telling you to get on the road," I said. Then I smiled archly. "It's still snowing, after all, and I wouldn't want to be accused of delaying you."

He eyed me, breathing hard. Then he made a move toward the kitchen, and I stepped into his path. "Can't I even give Mom a hug goodbye?" he said.

"No."

For a moment, I thought he'd knock me aside. Instead, he called out, in a much less combative tone of voice, "I'm gonna hit the road, Mom. I'll see you next week."

"Bye, dear," Mom called.

With a final glare at me, he stomped out the door.

I waited, listening to him start his SUV, knock snow off the windshield, and back out of the drive. When I was sure he was gone, I went into the kitchen. Mom hadn't moved, but her expression had cleared. "Why, hello, Maggie," she said with a pleased smile. "I didn't hear you come in."

I smiled back at her. "You know me, Mom. Sneaky." I pointed to the papers in front of her. "What's that?"

She looked down and turned them over. Then she shook her head. "I don't know," she said.

"Can I see them?" I held out my hand, and she gave them to me. It was only a couple of sheets of paper. The first page said QUITCLAIM DEED across the top. I was no legal expert, but it looked as if someone had printed a blank form from a website and hand-written stuff in the blanks – stuff that would give Mom's house to my brother and his wife.

I knew Mom had a will, because I had a copy, and I knew it made Sandy and me equal beneficiaries. When Mom died, we were to each get half of everything. Including the house.

"Did you tell Sandy you'd sell the house to him?" I asked, keeping my tone as neutral as possible.

Mom laughed. "What? No. That's crazy."

I laughed, too. "I'm just going to hold onto this. Is that okay?"

"Sure," she said. "What's for dinner? I could eat a horse!"

"Me, too," I said. "Lunch was a long time ago. What did you have?"

She paused. "I don't remember."

The storm didn't let up until nearly bedtime. I decided to spend the night with Mom, to give the road crews time to dig us out. I did go out after supper and move my car into the driveway, and I also shoveled the sidewalk . I figured I'd shovel out the drive in the morning. I'd just have to do it again after the plow came through, anyway.

I'd had two nights in my own bed, and now here I was, sleeping away from home again. Although this bed had been mine long before. Unlike Ruth and Arnie, Mom and Dad hadn't bothered with a wholesale redecorating effort after Sandy and I moved out. They had freshened up the paint throughout the house, and Mom had sewn new drapes, sticking to the pink-and-green decorating scheme we'd always had. But my bedroom was still a bedroom. Sandy's room, however, had become a general junk room. It was right next to the pull-down attic ladder, and Mom and Dad had had a habit of putting stuff meant for the attic in Sandy's old room "temporarily" – a habit that Mom had continued after Dad passed.

I said goodnight to Mom and shut the door to my room. Then I sat on the edge of the bed and, for the first time in hours, contemplated my own situation.

I needed to get busy and find a job. My savings weren't going to last much longer. Right now, I didn't have enough to put gas in my car and pay next month's rent. I supposed some retail store might hire me for the holidays, but that would only be short term – and the pay wouldn't be anything like what I'd been making at the casino. I needed a more permanent solution.

I looked around this mostly-empty room and wondered whether all my stuff would fit in it. It wouldn't be the first time in my adult life that I'd moved home, and just like the last time, it wouldn't be for long – just until I could get back on my feet financially. Mom might even enjoy having me around more. And I'd be able to keep a better eye on her.

I decided to suggest it to her in the morning.

Chapter 4

The next morning brought another crisis. Mom couldn't wake up.

She had always been the first person out of bed in the morning. She'd make coffee and eggs for Dad and get him out the door, and then get Sandy and me up and off to school. You know – Mom things. I did the same with my own family before I divorced Gene.

But this time, I was the first one up. Dawn was breaking as I got the coffee going. Then I went in to check on my mother. She was fast asleep, and no amount of poking, shaking, or shifting of her covers produced more than a groan.

After ten or so minutes of this, I sat on the edge of her bed, near tears. Then I spied the prescription bottle on her nightstand. It was the one Sandy had brought over the day before – the one he and Diane had had filled for her in Indianapolis. I opened the container and counted the pills inside. She had taken three.

Fear clutched my gut. I ran to the living room, picked up the landline phone, and dialed 911. Then, for good measure, I called Dr. Malik's office. His answering service assured me that he would meet us at the emergency room.

As the paramedics arrived, Dr. Malik himself called. "I just picked up your message," he said. "I'm at the hospital right now, doing rounds. Have the E.R. staff page me when you arrive."

"Okay," I said.

"And Maggie, do me a favor," he went on. "Bring in the bottle of pills she took. All right?"

"Yes, of course. It's already in my purse."

"Excellent. See you in a few minutes."

By this time, the paramedics had her on the stretcher and were heading out to the ambulance. I had a nerve-wracking drive behind them on the slippery streets.

The E.R. staff wouldn't let me stay with Mom while they pumped out her stomach, which – to be honest – I was okay with. I took a seat in the waiting room and settled in.

Presently, someone in scrubs led me back to the pod where Mom, bleary-eyed, lay on a gurney. Dr. Malik was there, talking to her quietly. I heard her say, "Sure." Then she saw me and frowned. He looked at her, and then at me.

"Hi," I said, and shook hands with the doctor. "Mom, how are you feeling?"

She opened her mouth, but Dr. Malik answered for her. "She's fine," he said, "but her throat's going to be sore for a few days because of the tube."

She nodded and pointed at her throat. I patted her hand in sympathy. Then I fished the pill bottle out of my purse and handed it over to the doctor.

He frowned as he read the label. "Where did she get this?"

"You know I was gone for a couple of months," I began.

"Aha," he said. "That explains why your mother missed an appointment with me. I wondered what was going on."

"I had to help an old friend with a problem," I said, looking pointedly at Mom and daring her to contradict me. Neither of us would typically describe Ruth as an old friend. Mom looked baffled, so I went on. "It ended up taking longer than I expected. Didn't my brother call to cancel?"

"No," he said. "And we do have to charge for the no-show."

"Of course," I said automatically, making a note to tell my brother that his so-called responsible behavior had cost Mom fifty bucks. "Anyway, she ended up staying with my brother and his wife in Indianapolis. I guess they took her to a doctor there."

"What did you think of Dr. Grayson, Mrs. Muir?" he asked Mom. She shrugged and shook her head.

"She's been having a lot of memory problems," I said.

"Well, I imagine it's been stressful for her with you gone. Older folks like to keep to their schedules."

"You think that's all it is?" I asked. "Just stress?" Stress had caused Ruth to have memory problems, too. But she'd had cancer, and she'd been keeping an ugly secret about her son – one that had caused her husband to kill himself.

"I think so," he said. "We'll keep an eye on her and see if her memory improves, now that you're back. But I'm going to advise you to dispose of this prescription. In fact, I'm going to make sure the E.R. staff disposes of it before you go."

"Wow. Okay," I said. "Why?"

"Dr. Grayson must not have asked for her medical history before he prescribed the Xanax for her," he said.

"I just wanted to go home," Mom croaked. "And that nurse asked me questions so fast, I couldn't answer them."

"What is Xanax?" I asked.

"It's a benzodiazepine." At my blank look, he elaborated, "A tranquilizer. They knock you out. And your mother is already taking another drug for that."

Something clicked in my mind. "Elavil, right?" I had seen an old bottle of it, with Arnie's name on it, in Ruth's medicine cabinet. I knew I'd seen the name somewhere, but couldn't place it at the time. Now I remembered where I'd seen it before: in Mom's medicine cabinet.

"Right," he said. "Amitriptyline. It's a tricyclic – an older type of antidepressant. It's also prescribed for anxiety and sleep disorders."

"She's been taking it for years, hasn't she?"

"Right again. I first prescribed it for her after your father died."

"I missed him," Mom said. "Couldn't sleep. The pills help."

"Is that why you took three of those Xanax?" I asked.

Her eyes widened. "I only took one!" she said, then winced and coughed.

"Well, there were three missing, and I couldn't wake you up this morning," I said. "That's why we're here."

She looked at the IV in her hand. "Oh," she said in a small voice. Then, "Can I go home now?"

"Pretty soon," said Dr. Malik. "The doctors and nurses here want to make sure you're stable before they send you home." To me, he said, "Call my office and make an appointment for her for tomorrow, would you? And make a note of any prescription meds you see around the house. Better yet, bring them all in. I want to make sure nobody else is prescribing medications for your mother."

"Sure, no problem," I said.

"When can I go home?" Mom asked. "I'm starving."

Mom seemed more with it after we left the emergency room. Still, I decided to stay over at her house for another night. I'd gotten dressed that morning in the clothes I'd worn the day before, since I hadn't expected to stay over. So we stopped by my place on the way home so I could change, bring in my own groceries (the cold stuff was still in Mom's fridge), and pack a bag for one more night. I put out some of the crackers and fruit I'd just bought, as Mom had said she was so hungry, but she only picked at them.

Her appetite was a little better at lunchtime, but not much. She had soup and coffee, and then went down for a nap. I supposed all the excitement that morning had worn her out – and I hoped the E.R. excursion didn't make her more forgetful.

Supper was much the same – Mom ate very lightly and then dozed in front of the TV for a while. I used the time to check her room and the bathroom for pill containers, but I didn't find any prescription meds other than the amitriptyline.

She really did seem to be sleeping a lot, and by suppertime, she had no recollection of the trip to the E.R. – or of stopping by my apartment in the afternoon. I felt like I was out of my depth. It had been easier to deal with Ruth's occasional forays into confusion – she was with it most of the time, even though she was also cranky most of the time.

So when my daughter Bea, the psychologist, happened to call that evening, I was grateful to bend her ear with my troubles. "It's just frustrating," I said, after explaining about Mom's forgetfulness. "I feel like I should never have gone to Rockville."

"Well, *I'm* glad you came," said Bea. "And so are Royce and Ryker. Royce especially misses you a lot."

That gave me a warm, fuzzy feeling. "I miss her, too. I miss all of you. And I really am glad I went." The trip had allowed Bea and me to reconnect. She hadn't spoken to me since before the divorce was final. "It's just…"

"You feel guilty that you took time for yourself."

"Yeah. I guess that's it."

"Where's that guilt trip coming from?"

I paused. "What do you mean? Are you saying I'm beating myself up for no good reason?"

"No, I'm saying you're beating yourself up for *some* reason, and you should figure out what it is so you can stop doing it."

I chuckled. "Ah, okay. That makes more sense."

"So who bought your ticket for the guilt train?"

"Your uncle Sandy," I said immediately.

"Oh? You spoke to him?"

"He was here," I said. And then I launched into the story of his surprise visit, and the prescription Diane had gotten for Mom, and the subsequent emergency room trip.

"Wait," said Bea. "Aunt Diane took Grandma to a different doctor? What's wrong with the one she has?"

"He's Muslim," I said with a sigh.

"And?"

"That's it. Something something sharia law."

"Oh my God," said Bea. "He can't be serious. Does Aunt Diane agree with him?"

"I didn't get an opportunity to talk religion with her," I said, letting the sarcasm flow. "She criticized me for having a lead foot, so I hung up on her."

"I have no idea what that means, but good for you," she said. "And he's nuts, by the way. John says some of the smartest physicians he works with are Muslim."

"I believe you – and John. I have no complaints about Dr. Malik. But your uncle believes my misplaced faith is just another example of how I'm not taking care of Grandma properly. He said it was irresponsible of me to take off and not have anyone here to watch her."

"*He* was supposed to be watching her."

"That's what I told him. Oh – and he's trying to get Mom to deed her house to him."

"What?"

I explained about the DIY quitclaim deed. "Which reminds me," I said, "I need to run that thing by a lawyer, and see if there's any way to block him from trying anything like it again."

"Mom, things aren't adding up here," she said. "Why would he want Grandma's house? Don't he and Aunt Diane own their place in Indianapolis?"

"They do. I don't understand it myself. Maybe he needs money and he's already mortgaged his own place to the hilt." I laughed shortly. "If that's the case, though, the joke will be on him. He's not going to get nearly as much out of Grandma's house as he could his own. Home values are a lot lower here."

"Mom," she said. "I'm starting to think you should move in with Grandma."

I sighed. "I'm starting to think so, too. My savings are running a bit low, and I don't know how long it'll take for me to find another job."

"If you need help…" she began.

I shut her down. "That's very sweet of you, Bea, but I wouldn't take money from you and John if I were destitute. You two have your own little family to provide for. Don't you worry about me. I've managed things pretty well for the past fifty-eight years. I'll be fine."

"I know you will," she said, backing off. "So tomorrow?"

"Tomorrow," I said, "Grandma goes to see the doctor in the morning. Then in the afternoon, I need to update my resume and start looking for a job."

"And call a lawyer."

"Right. That, too." I added it to my mental to-do list. "Thanks for calling and letting me vent, sweetie."

"It's what I do," she said with a laugh. "Next time, I'll call when the kids are awake. They'd love to chat with you. And I bet Grandma would get a kick out of it, too."

"I'm sure she would," I said. "That's a great idea. Let's do it soon."

Chapter 5

And so it went for the next week or so. I spent my mornings squiring Mom around town, to the doctor, or the grocery store, or the senior center for some activity or another. The folks at the senior center were thrilled to see her. They all said they'd been worried about her when she stopped coming. One of her friends said, "Shirley, why didn't you call me if you needed a ride? I would have picked you up!"

"I honestly did not think of it, Mavis," Mom said.

"Well, think of it next time," Mavis said. "It's not nice to worry us by dropping off the face of the earth like that. At our age, there's no telling why people quit showing up. Could be they're on vacation, could be they're not driving any more – or it could be the big ol' dirt nap." She laughed uproariously, and Mom laughed with her.

As I drove away, I thought how different Mom's golden years were from Ruth's. My ex-mother-in-law spent her days watching TV from her recliner. The only time she ever got out of the house was for a doctor appointment or to see family. Mom, on the other hand, had a real social life.

Part of it was age – Ruth was older than my mother – but part of it was temperament. Ruth wasn't a pleasant person, generally speaking, and my mother was.

Even so, I thought about suggesting to Ruth that she check out the list of activities at her local senior center. Even if she didn't make any friends, at least she wouldn't be cooped up in that house all the time.

And then I thought about her likely reaction and dropped the whole idea.

Anyway, my mornings were devoted to Mom and my afternoons were spent scanning the job listings. They were pretty sparse. I might have some luck after the holidays with a tax-preparing job, based on my work experience at the casino, but right now they weren't hiring. Even holiday-related retail jobs were thin on the ground. Most places, it turned out, had staffed up in September and early October, while I was in Maryland – and from what I could tell, most stores didn't hire like they had in the past. Local retail seemed to be dying out as more and more people shopped online.

With that realization, I even applied for seasonal jobs with the U.S. Postal Service and some of the big shipping operations. But none of them seemed interested in hiring a fifty-eight-year-old woman who hadn't done much heavy lifting in her life prior to this.

I might have had better luck if I'd been willing to relocate. Cincinnati, Louisville, and Indianapolis were all within a few hours' drive of Lawrenceburg, but every time I thought of being that far away from Mom, I just couldn't do it. Not with her health the way it was. Now, don't get me wrong – she wasn't failing, as Sandy had tried to say. But her memory did come and go, even after life got back to an even keel.

The staff at the senior center noticed it. Well, she kind of made them notice it. A few days before Christmas, the director pulled me aside and said, "I wanted you to know that we're a little concerned about Shirley. We think she may be suffering from dementia."

I frowned. "I know she's having some memory problems," I said. "I've talked with Dr. Malik about it, too."

"Well, just so you know," she said. "She's wandered away twice – once last week, and then again today. She'll get up to use the bathroom and not come back. This morning, we found her a block away without her coat."

"Oh," I said, my stomach dropping. It had been in the thirties for most of the morning. "Oh, no. I had no idea."

"Well, that's why I'm telling you," she said. She pulled a brochure from a stand near the door and handed it to me. "Catholic Charities runs a day program for people with memory problems in Cincinnati. You might want to look into enrolling her there."

I blinked. "That's quite a drive."

"I know," she said. "And I'm sorry about that, but I just don't think this program is suitable for her any more. Our facility isn't secure enough to handle Alzheimer's patients, and our staff isn't trained for it, either." I must have looked bereft, because she patted my arm. "I'm not saying you can't ever bring her here again. We'll do what we can for her while you look for another solution. But you should probably start looking now, with the aim of moving her into the new program after the holidays."

"Thanks," I said. "Thanks for telling me." I stuffed the brochure in my purse and left the building.

"Great," I muttered as I got in my car. "Just great. Here, let me add that to my to-do list." I had intended to go home and clean up my apartment, but nothing seemed less appealing. Instead, I drove aimlessly, turning when the mood struck me and letting the car go where it would. I wasn't even looking at the scenery, really; I was just driving to drive.

Eventually, I began to pay attention again, and I realized I knew where I was. I had driven to the part of the county where Mom, Dad, Sandy, and I had lived before my parents bought the house in Lawrenceburg. I'd been little when we moved away, but I recognized the name of the street where we'd lived, and then found the lot where our house trailer had stood. The trailer was gone, which didn't surprise me; it had been old when we lived in it. The people next door had apparently bought the lot and put up a gazebo, complete with a shaded fishpond that sported a fast-melting skim of ice.

The place appeared deserted, and there was no traffic. I parked my car off the road, locked my purse in the trunk, and got out to take a walk.

As soon as I got out of the car, I could feel my turtle dancing on its chain. I pulled it out from under my shirt and let it rest against my coat, where it calmed. But it had a different air about it than usual. Alert, maybe. Or expectant.

I shook my head at the fanciful notion and headed off the road, down a well-worn game path that I'd chased Sandy and his friends down many times. Of course, everything was much bigger in my memory – the trees, the width of the path, and especially the distances. In a much shorter period of time than my three-year-old self would have thought possible, I came upon the spot where I'd found the turtle.

I'd been angry at the boys that day, and kicked at the ground in frustration. I had always assumed my fortuitous kick had dislodged the thing from the dirt – but now I wasn't so sure. I was more attuned to the turtle's messages now than I had been as a child, and it seemed to me that it hadn't found what it was looking for in this place. This, I was sure, wasn't our destination.

I crouched at the approximate place where I'd picked up the turtle and murmured, "Where do you want to go?"

As if in reply, I felt a very strong pull on my left side – not enough to knock me off-balance, but strong enough to be sure there was no other explanation.

"Okay," I said, struggling to my feet as my knees creaked in protest. "Left it is."

We meandered in the woods for probably fifteen or twenty minutes, getting closer and closer to the fence that separated the woods from the fallow field beyond. I began to worry that the turtle would expect me to climb between the lines of barbed wire – which was not going to happen – and then I began to be concerned about the amount of time this was taking. I had to be back at the senior center to pick up Mom at 11:45 a.m. If we didn't wrap up this search in another five minutes or so, the turtle and I were going to have to complete this quest another day.

As if in answer to my concerns, I stopped feeling pulled in any direction. The change was so abrupt that I stumbled a little, and went down on one knee. And then I looked at the patch of land I was kneeling on, and sank to a seated position in – shock? Reverence? Recognition? For there before me, obscured by snow, frosty leaf mold, and undergrowth, was the outline of a burial mound.

It had been perhaps twenty-five feet in diameter. The mound itself was gone, but a slight depression showed there had been a ditch around its base, and a raised earthwork surrounding the ditch. This had been a sacred site, then – not just a burial mound, but possibly a ceremonial site, as well.

I got to my feet and dodged dried vegetation to make my way to the center of the circle. There, I closed my eyes.

Sadness overcame me. I heard weeping. And then I was above the crowd, hovering, as a shaman wearing brass-antlered headgear cried out in words whose meaning echoed in my bones: the sacrifice one makes for one's people is critical to the health of the earth. For it is in renewing one another that the earth itself is renewed.

Then fire! The reek of burning flesh filled my nostrils.

I gasped and opened my eyes. I'd just witnessed my own funeral.

My people weren't barbarians; it was clear I'd been dead before my body was set alight. I sensed no fear or horror, no violence – so my sacrifice didn't involve losing my life. Instead, I felt that it had to do with what I had done with my life: how I'd lived, not how I'd died.

My turtle had begun to glow – a clean red-gold, the color of sunrise. But then it darkened, and I sensed I was about to learn more.

Years had passed. My people had moved on and my tomb had been abandoned to the forest. Then a man came along. He was dressed in homespun and carried a hoe; he aimed to farm this piece of rocky land, and my burial mound was in his way. So he began to hack at the side of the mound.

I hated that man. I hated that he refused to leave me in peace. I wanted to rise up and snatch the hoe from his hands, and break the handle over his head. Or take a hoe to the resting places of his own loved ones. This was desecration! This was...

Abruptly, I was back again in the present day. That man in homespun – the one my spirit had cursed for desecrating my tomb – had farmed this land hundreds of years ago. I could find his descendants, maybe, and somehow rain doom upon them for the actions of their ancestor. But what was the point? The descendants wouldn't know why they had been cursed.

I would be making them suffer for something they couldn't have done anything about.

The turtle's dirty light abruptly went out.

I looked down at it, confused. I'd discovered that if I made some progress in my journey, some of the green-black tarnish on the turtle would melt away – but if I made a wrong turn, it would somehow re-tarnish itself. Neither appeared to be happening just now. It had simply gone out.

I'd been assuming all along that the turtle was guiding me on my path. But maybe it was only taking me where it wanted to go. Now that I'd decided not to help it, maybe it had deserted me.

I sighed. It was getting late, and I was suddenly cold. I didn't know how long I'd been out here, but I suspected I wouldn't make it back in time to pick up Mom – which meant another black mark against me with the senior center staff, who were already suggesting Mom needed to be in a different program elsewhere.

With a heavy heart, I turned to retrace my steps...

And something pinged against my boot.

I bent over to look at it. It, too, was copper, and as dirty-looking as the turtle effigy had been at first. But this was flat, and it was in the shape of a bird.

As I picked it up, my turtle began to buzz frantically. This, too, had been mine in that long-ago time. Both of these effigies had been buried with me, and now I had them back.

My feelings of failure flew away. This was what I had been brought here to find.

I made my way back to the car much more rapidly than I would have thought possible. Inside, with the heater blasting, my cold fingers fumbled at the clasp of my necklace until at last, I got it off. Then with shaking hands, I threaded the chain through holes high in the bird's back and pushed the new effigy down until it lay against and partly behind the turtle.

Both of them lit up. It almost seemed as if the turtle's light flowed into the bird where they touched, and some of the bird's tarnish disappeared. Then the light went out.

I put the necklace on again and tucked it under my shirt. Then I looked at the clock on the dashboard. And looked again. And checked what it said against my phone. It seemed impossible, but only five minutes had passed since I had parked the car.

I pulled away, feeling exhilarated. I still didn't have a job and Mom was still losing touch with reality. Heck, maybe I was losing touch with reality myself. But I had a bird to go with my turtle, and it felt like I'd accomplished something big.

Chapter 6

I felt like celebrating, even if I was the only one who knew what the celebration was for. So I picked up something special on the way to get Mom. She had stayed put that day, thank goodness, so I didn't have to suffer through the senior center director giving me the stinkeye.

"What's that heavenly scent?" Mom asked when she got in the car. "Smells like fried chicken!"

"I had a little extra time today," I said with a grin.

She clapped her hands in excitement. "Oh, I just love fried chicken! I used to make it every Sunday for dinner, with mashed potatoes. Did you get mashed potatoes, too?"

"Of course I did. Wouldn't be fried chicken without mashed potatoes."

"Bless your heart. You think of everything." She gave me her proud-mom smile. Then she sobered. "But I'll pay you back. You shouldn't be spending money on restaurant food, what with not having a job."

"I have an idea about that," I said. "Let's talk about it when we get home."

Settled at last around the kitchen table, we chomped through our chicken and sides for a few moments. Mom's appetite was better than usual. I wondered whether she was just bored with her regular meal choices. Maybe I could try to change it up now and then – which would be easier if I weren't living across town.

I put down my fork and said, "I had an idea that I wanted to run past you."

"Shoot," she said, as she gnawed a little more meat from a wing bone.

"I took a look at my savings account a little while ago," I said. "It's getting pretty low."

She put down the wing and leaned in. "Do you need help?" she asked in a confidential tone – as if anyone else was around to hear her. "I've got lots of money. Your father left me pretty well fixed."

"No. I mean, that's not what I'm asking," I said. "I figure I'll find a new job pretty soon. Something part-time, at least. No, what worries me is making the rent in a couple of weeks."

"Why don't you move in with me?"

"Actually," I said, beginning to smile, "that's what I was going to suggest."

She went on as if she needed to sell me on the idea. "I mean, you're here half the time anyway. You could have your old room back, just like when you were here before. And I'd be happy to have the company."

"You would?" I said, surprised.

"Well, sure," she said. "It's been too quiet around here since your father died. I get kind of tired of looking at the same four walls all day."

"But you have your friends at the senior center," I said.

She gave me a sad smile. "They're not the same as family. And you heard Mavis – you never know when someone's going to leave and never come back. Makes it hard to keep a friendship going."

I could see that.

She went on, "The only reason I'm close to Mavis is because her daughter Janie was in the same class as Sandy in elementary school. And it's not like we're best pals or anything." She sat for a moment, lost in thought. "I haven't had a best pal since your father died."

My heart went out to her. It had been a long time since I'd had a best pal, too. It was before I married Gene, for sure, and that was more than thirty years ago.

"I'd be happy to be your best pal," I said, blinking back tears.

"Well," she said. "That would be just fine."

We sat and smiled at each other like idiots for a few minutes.

Then Mom started putting lids on the leftovers. "Now, don't go to the expense of hiring movers," she said, as I stacked our plates. "We'll call Sandy and get him and Diane to come down and help."

Immediately, I had second thoughts about the whole scheme. "He's got a bad back, Mom. I don't want him to hurt himself. Maybe Bea and John can come. And you could see your grandkids then – wouldn't that be great?" I smiled encouragingly.

Mom had not lost her touch with the annoyed-mom stare. "Call your brother, Margaret."

Ouch. Even when you're nearly sixty years old, when your mother uses your full first name, you know you're in trouble. So I sucked it up and called my brother.

I used Mom's landline in the living room. Diane picked up, but didn't have anything to say to me except "Hello?" and "Just a minute." A few seconds later, Sandy picked up.

"What do you want?" was his opening salvo.

"Hello to you, too," I said. "Nice to talk to you again. I guess you got home okay the other night."

"Just cut the crap, Maggie. What do you want?"

"I'm giving up my apartment and moving in with Mom. She said I should call and ask you to drive down here and help me."

"Oh, *hell* no."

"No, you won't come and help? Or…?"

"No, you are *not* moving in with Mom. Over my dead body."

That can be arranged was on the tip of my tongue, but it didn't sound like he was in the mood for a joke. "You don't have any control over what I do."

"But I control the house, and I'm forbidding you from moving in."

"Since when do you control the house?" I asked, incredulous.

"Mom signed a quitclaim deed while I was there that last time," he said, a note of triumph in his voice. "She signed the whole place over to me. She can keep living there for a while, of course. But *you* do *not* have my permission to live there."

I remembered, belatedly, the two-page fill-in-the-blanks deed I'd found on the kitchen table after he left. With everything else that had been going on, I'd forgotten to find a lawyer to look at it.

He took my silence as permission to plow ahead, I guess. "You're nearly sixty years old, Maggie. I'm not going to let you freeload off of Mom and spend all her money. You need to get off your dead ass and find yourself a *job*."

I found my voice at last. "I'm *looking* for a job. But I haven't found one yet. It's difficult for someone my age to get hired. And there aren't a ton of jobs here to begin with."

"Then maybe you shouldn't have lost your last job," he sneered. "Maybe you shouldn't have gone gallivanting off to the East Coast and left Mom alone!"

"You were supposed to be taking care of her!" I said. But it was a weak comeback, and I knew it. With every word he said, I felt smaller and more pathetic. Had I really screwed up my life that badly? I felt like I'd always done what I had to do. Life gave me lemons a lot of the time; maybe I didn't always make lemonade with them, but I always survived. But my decisions all sounded stupider when he described them.

He plowed ahead relentlessly. "Mom's had quite enough of your tender, loving care. What she needs is to get out of that little one-horse town. She needs to live in a place where she'll be taken care of as she gets older and her health gets worse. And she needs a decent doctor – one that speaks English."

I bristled at the veiled insult to Dr. Malik. "All of which – let me guess – she can have in Indianapolis," I said.

"Diane is looking into assisted living places for her. She'll be with people her own age. She'll have friends galore! And she'll be right near us."

I was about to reply that Mom had friends right here, including me – but Mom herself moved into my field of vision. She held out one hand and commanded, "Give me that phone." So I did.

"Alexander Elmer Muir," she said. "You need to stop this foolishness right now. Your sister needs your help. Get down here and help her!" Then she listened, growing increasingly slack-jawed. I could hear Sandy ranting at her, but I couldn't hear what he said. At last, she said goodbye and put the handset back in its cradle. She turned to me and said dully, "He's not going to come."

"I never thought he would," I said.

She lowered herself slowly to the sofa and perched on the edge of the cushions, staring out the picture window, with her back rounded and her forearms on her knees. She looked as if one touch would splinter her into a thousand pieces.

"I'm sorry," I said.

"It's not your fault." She still wouldn't look at me.

"Mom." I paused. "When Sandy was here the other day, he brought some papers with him. I saw them sitting on the kitchen table after he left. Remember?"

"Sure," she said, her tone flat.

"Did you sign anything? I have the paperwork he left on the table – it's at my apartment. You didn't sign that one. But did you sign another copy? One that he might have taken with him?"

At last, she looked at me in anguish. "I don't remember."

I moved *call a lawyer* to the top of my mental to-do list.

It wasn't too late in the day to start looking for an attorney, but I felt defeated. Instead, I gave Mom a hug and got in my car to head home.

It suddenly hit me that Christmas was just two days away, and I had no tree and no plans. When we were kids, Mom and Dad always hosted on the big day. In the old days, Dad would have wrestled the tree and ornaments down the attic ladder by now; I'd be putting up the tree and decorating it while Mom started the pies. On the big day, we'd open gifts in the morning, and then Dad and Sandy would settle in to watch some sporting event in the living room, while Mom and I cooked. After Sandy got married, Diane would spend a little time helping Mom and me, and then wander off to watch some Christmas special on the smaller TV in Sandy's old room. When I moved back home after the divorce, I discovered Diane had begun hosting every year so her parents could come, too. So for the past few years, Mom and I had been driving up to Indianapolis to have dinner with people I wasn't related to. It seemed odd and uncomfortable to me. I much preferred sitting around the family table with people I loved.

This year, Mom might receive an invitation from Sandy and Diane, but I certainly didn't expect one. I decided it might be prudent to plan to fend for myself. I didn't care about the tree and I certainly didn't expect gifts from anyone. But I could pick up a turkey breast and some stuff to go with it, and if Mom ended up staying home, she could help me eat it. So I made a quick detour to the grocery store.

"Hi, Maggie!" Marty hollered as soon as I walked in. He was bagging groceries that day. I waved and started to grab a cart, but he motioned me over.

"Nice to see you," I said.

He was beaming. "Mr. Olsen told me to watch for you. He wants to talk to you." He nodded toward the staff shack in the front corner of the store, behind the customer service window. Then he went on in a sing-song voice, "I think it's good news."

"Is he in there now?" I asked.

"Yup!"

"Okay, then. Thanks," I said, and headed that way. Ron Olsen had been the store's general manager for the past several decades. I couldn't imagine what he wanted to talk to me about. It couldn't be a job; the grocery store was the one place where I hadn't dropped off a resume.

I knocked on the door that said *EMPLOYEES ONLY* and waited. In a minute, Ron opened the door and beckoned me in. "Good to see you, Maggie, good to see you," he said, pumping my hand. "I heard you had a bit of bad luck over at the casino."

"I don't know that I'd call it bad luck," I said. "I needed more time off than they were willing to give me."

His mouth quirked up on one side. "Right. Look. I've known you for years, and I know you would never speak badly of a former employer. But I also know your old boss at the casino. And Dee is not nearly as decent and honorable as you are."

My mouth fell open. Maybe it wasn't just my age that was keeping potential employers from calling me. "What's he been saying?"

"Let's just say it hasn't been complimentary," Ron said. "Look. As it happens, I'm short a shift manager. It doesn't pay quite what you were making at the casino" – he gave me a salary figure – "but it's full-time with benefits."

"As it happens," I said, "I'm in a position to entertain your offer, even though the salary is not what I'm used to."

"Good!" he said. "Glad that's settled. Come on in tomorrow morning at nine, and we'll get you to fill out all the paperwork."

And here was the first hurdle already. "Um. Could we make it nine-thirty? I have to drop Mom off at the senior center at nine."

He smiled broadly. "Whatever you need, Maggie, we'll make it work. You've always been an exemplary employee, and I'm more than happy to accommodate you."

We shook hands again. As I turned to go, I said, "Tell me. What did Dee do to you?"

Ron shouted a laugh. "Let's just say he's been poaching my best workers for years – including you. Now I'm in a position to poach one back. And I'm a much nicer guy to work for."

I grinned. "Yes, you are. Thanks, Ron."

I shot a thumbs-up to Marty as I left the shack; he insisted on a high-five, which I gave him. Then I nearly skipped around the store, picking up everything I'd need for a feast.

It wasn't until I was in the car on my way home that my mood faded. It dawned on me that I'd come full circle; once again, I was back at the same place where I'd worked in high school. This time, I'd be a manager, not a cashier. But I was sure my brother would figure out a way to spin it so that it would sound like I was a loser.

Chapter 7

My good mood had completely evaporated by the time I'd finished putting the groceries away. I'd done the math and realized that I really wasn't going to be able to afford this apartment any more. I had no alternative – I was going to have to move in with Mom, whether Sandy liked it or not.

I was so demoralized by the fight I knew I was going to have to have with him that I almost didn't answer the phone when it rang. But then I looked at the caller ID, and nearly dropped the phone in my haste to answer it. "Abby!" I said. "Am I glad you called!"

Abby Brandt – well, it was Abby Brandt-Walters now – was my ex-husband's youngest sister. We had bonded when I first moved to Maryland to the point where I felt closer to her than I did to Gene. She was several years younger than me, and had been trying for years to break into Hollywood: auditioning like crazy, picking up an acting job now and then, and mostly working retail jobs to keep from starving. Not long ago, she had married her girlfriend Sallie, and they had recently adopted a baby girl. "How's motherhood?" I asked now.

"Exhausting," she said. "But also exhilarating. Bernice is the best baby ever. Did you get the pictures I sent last week?"

"I did. She's adorable. I showed them to Mom, and she thought so, too."

"Did she…" She paused. "Did she know who we were? Sorry."

I sighed. "I think so. Sometimes it's hard to tell."

"How is that going, anyway?"

"Oh, just fine and dandy," I said sarcastically, and then told her the latest – about the prescription Diane had gotten for Mom, and how they wanted to move her to Indianapolis to be closer to them, and how they thought I was doing a lousy job as Mom's caretaker.

"I'd be able to keep an eye on her better if I lived with her," I finished, "but Sandy gave me some cockamamie story about how he owns the house now, and he doesn't want me living there."

"Why not?" she asked, indignant on my behalf.

"He thinks I'd be freeloading off of Mom. He told me I ought to get up off my butt and find a real job."

Abby called him a few colorful and inventive names that I would never repeat in polite society, but that had me laughing until I cried. "Okay, but seriously, Maggie," she said, "I bet he's bluffing. Have you seen a new deed or anything?"

I cast a glance toward the kitchen table, where the handwritten deed still sat. "Mom had something that claimed to be a deed, but I don't think it's legal. I keep meaning to find a lawyer to look it over, but it's been one thing after another here." I told her about Mom wandering off from the senior center, and about how the director wanted me to find another program for her. "Which I'm going to have tons of time to do, now that I'm starting a new job tomorrow."

"You got hired? That's fantastic! Congratulations!"

"Thanks," I said.

"You don't sound enthusiastic."

"It's at the grocery store where I worked when I was in high school," I confessed. "It's a manager position, so it pays more than just being a cashier. But I feel like I've come full circle to a place I wasn't nuts about being the first time."

"I hear you," Abby said. "Listen. What if we cheered you up with a visit?"

My eyes widened in pleasure. "That would be great! When?"

"How about for Christmas?" I could hear the grin in her voice. "I was actually calling to invite you here to spend the holidays with us. I know it's last minute and you're probably broke, but I figured you could use a vacation, and we've got miles saved up."

"That's very generous, Abby, but…"

"You can't get away. I got that part. But for once, Sallie can. She has the whole weekend off, from Thursday through Monday. So we could come see you."

"You guys must have a lot of miles," I said.

"A few." Her tone turned sly. "We could even help you move to your mom's, if you want. Your brother the asshole won't have to lift a finger. And good luck to him, throwing you out after you've already moved in."

"You're devious," I said. "I've always liked that about you."

"I do what I can," she said modestly.

"What about Bernice, though?" I asked. "Won't it be hard to travel with a baby?"

"She's actually a perfect age for it," she said, "as long as we can get her to sleep during the flight."

I thought of another potential issue. "Won't your mother be upset that you're coming here for the holidays, instead of going home?" The Brandts were Jewish, but Ruth always ordered a turkey from Magruder's for Christmas Eve. I considered it bribery to get me to bring the kids to her house for every night of Hanukkah.

"Mom can just get over herself," Abby declared, and I giggled. "To be honest, I don't know what the family is doing this year. I think maybe Bea's hosting."

"Not Riley?" I thought Gene's second wife would have taken over the big meal prep – maybe because it's what I would have done.

"Things are a little delicate there," said Abby.

"Oh? Bea didn't say anything when I spoke with her."

"She may not have known. Riley kicked Gene out."

I blinked. "The house was in his name, I thought."

"That's what I thought, too."

"How could she kick him out, then?"

"You got me," Abby said. "All Ma said was that Riley'd had enough of Gene's shenanigans and threw him out. He's staying at Ma's now, sleeping in his old room in the basement."

A sudden thought occurred to me. "Is Debbie still there?"

"My mind went there, too," she said with a knowing laugh. "No, she went back home before Riley kicked Gene out."

I shook my head, thinking of all I'd set in motion when I insisted on getting to the bottom of the Brandt family secrets.

"Anyway," she went on, "the last thing I want to do is step into that mess. I'd rather spend a nice, uncomplicated Christmas with you and Sallie and Bernice and your mom."

I couldn't help laughing. "I'm afraid uncomplicated isn't on the menu this year. But I'd love to see you, and I won't turn down the help with the move."

"Deal," she said. "We'll probably fly in on Thursday morning. I'll email you our flight info when I get it." She squealed. "I can't wait to see you!"

"It's been way too long," I agreed.

"And Maggie? Seriously. Get a lawyer to look at that deed. He's bluffing – I feel it in my bones. But better safe than sorry."

"I promise," I said. "See you Friday." I ended the call and looked around the apartment, feeling more energetic than I had in a while. "Guess I'd better start packing."

When I picked Mom up the next morning, I told her Abby had called. "Who's Abby?" Mom said.

"Gene's sister," I said carefully, in case it was the dementia talking. "The one in California."

"Oh."

"She married another woman and they have a baby girl."

She quirked an eyebrow at me. "It didn't use to work that way."

I laughed. "They had a surrogate mother for the baby. Her name is Bernice."

"Whose name?"

"The baby's name." I wanted to laugh, but I didn't want to insult my mother. It wasn't her fault her memory was going.

"What's her... What's the other mother's name?"

"Abby's wife's name is Sallie. And they're going to be here Friday for Christmas."

Mom looked at me in surprise. "Christmas is Friday? But I don't have a turkey! And I haven't bought presents for anyone! The tree's still up in the attic!"

"It's okay, Mom," I said, soothing her. "Abby and Sallie aren't going to expect gifts from us, and I don't want anything from you. And besides, I bought all the food yesterday."

"But we need to make pies. We should have done that last night!" She looked at me anxiously. "We'll just have to make them tonight. Did you get any mincemeat?"

My heart turned over. The only person in our family who would eat mincemeat pie was my father. "I didn't need to. Dad's gone."

"But he'll be home tonight," she said. "After work."

"No, Mom, he died."

She looked at me for a moment, chin trembling. Then she looked out the window and didn't say anything else.

As I pulled into the senior center parking lot, my mind was miles away, thinking of everything I needed to do that day: stop by the store to fill out paperwork, pick up any boxes they hadn't crushed yet, start packing, and find a lawyer. I intended to just let Mom out at the curb, but my turtle began vibrating inside my coat.

"What's that buzzing noise?" Mom asked. It was the first time she'd spoken since her confusion over Dad being gone.

"It's an alarm," I said.

"What's it for?"

"I don't know yet. Come on – I'll walk you in."

The senior center was usually pretty quiet, but that morning, there was a low-frequency hum that I hadn't sensed before. "What's going on?" I asked the receptionist.

"Didn't you see the notice on the board last week?" she asked.

"No," I began.

But she had just kept talking. "We have some people here today from the Legal Aid Society. They're helping clients with wills and powers of attorney. That kind of thing."

I pulled out my phone to check the time. Nope, there wasn't enough time for me to run home, get the DIY deed Sandy had left at Mom's, bring it back here, and still make it to the store by nine-thirty. And I couldn't be late on my first day of work, no matter how accommodating Ron said he'd be. "How long will they be here?"

"Just until noon," she said.

I had no idea how long Ron would need to keep me. "Maybe I'll just poke my head in and see if one of them has a business card."

"Of course," she said.

"Do you need me to come with you?" Mom asked.

"No, I'm fine. Go on to your exercise class."

She didn't need to be told twice. "See you later, Maggie," she said as I gave her a hug. *At least she hasn't forgotten me again, even if she did forget Dad was dead.*

Now, at last, I noticed the sign that said LEGAL AID CLINIC on the conference room door. I strode toward it, and nearly collided with a man who was coming from the kitchen with a cup of coffee. We both backed up and said, nearly simultaneously, "Oh! Are you all right? Yes, I'm fine."

I handed him a tissue to blot up the coffee that had sloshed over his hand. As he attended to that, I got a good look at him. "Jinx," I said with a grin. "You owe me a soda."

"Pardon?"

I laughed. "Rick, it's me. Maggie Muir."

It was his turn to laugh. "Why, Maggie May! I didn't recognize you."

Rick Hughes had aged very well. His hair was grayer – and much shorter – than it had been in high school in the '70s, but then so was mine. We were both considered bright – I guess those kids are called nerds now – and we both went to Indiana University after graduation, but he went on to law school, and of course I got pregnant and dropped out. He'd worked for a top law firm in Indy, but I'd heard he had moved home to Lawrenceburg at about the same time my father died.

"So what are you up to these days, Maggie May?" he asked. I remembered that cocky smile.

"Not much," I hedged. "Just dropping off my mom for her exercise class. But I'm glad I ran into you. How late will you be here today? I have some papers that I need a lawyer to look over."

"For you or for your mom? The clinic today is for seniors, and I know you don't qualify."

"Flattery will get you nowhere," I said dryly. "No, it's for Mom. It's kind of a long story, actually."

"And you don't have the documents with you."

"Of course not. And I have an appointment at nine-thirty, so I can't run home to get it."

"Tell you what." He set his cup down on a nearby table so he could pull out a business card. "I can probably work you into my schedule this afternoon. Call me on my cell when you've attended to your business, and we'll figure out a time that works for us both."

"Thanks, Rick." I stuck his card in my coat pocket. "I'm so glad I ran into you today."

"Things happen for a reason," he said, with an odd smile.

Under my blouse, the turtle warmed slightly. "Yes, they do," I said.

Ron wasn't at the store when I got there, but he had left me a welcome memo and a packet of forms to fill out. I got my old mail slot back, and my old locker, which was both comforting and a little depressing.

Managers' uniforms – a vest-and-slacks ensemble with a long-sleeved shirt – were different than what the cashiers wore, and Ron said in his note that he had already put in the order for some in my size; I had to wear a white shirt with my old uniform pants until the new duds came in. Schedules always ran Monday-to-Sunday, so my first official day on the payroll wouldn't be until after the holiday weekend. Which was perfect – I would have plenty of time to visit with Abby and Sallie, and move to Mom's, too.

Everyone on the staff seemed glad I was back, and nobody seemed upset that I was getting promoted to manager, even though I hadn't been there as long as many of them had. Marty insisted on giving me several high-fives. "You know I'm not going to go easy on you, right?" I said. "Don't think I'm going to let you get away with anything just because you're being nice to me now."

"Aw, Maggie. You're always nice."

"You think so? Ask my kids. I think they may have a different opinion."

All of that took me until lunchtime. I drove home, found the stupid deed, and called Rick on my cell phone.

To my surprise, he picked up. "Maggie May. I was just wondering when you'd call."

"You must be psychic," I said. "Are you still holding court at the senior center?"

"Nope. Just finished up. Have you had lunch?"

"Not yet," I said. And then, for no good reason, I added, "Are you asking me out, Mr. Hughes?"

"Strictly business, Ms. Muir," he said. "I'll write it off on my taxes. Where would you like to go?"

"Something nicer than Steak & Shake," I said with a grin. "Since you're writing it off, and all."

"How about Whisky's?"

"Sounds great," I said. "I need to pick up Mom and drop her off at her house, so…"

"Why don't you bring her along? The documents concern her, don't they?"

"They do. Okay, sure. We'll meet you there in about half an hour."

Rick beat us there. And he must have bribed the waitress, as he was sitting at a table in a corner far from the rest of the lunch crowd. "Good to see you both, Mrs. Muir, Ms. Muir," he said. He gallantly held the chair out for Mom and helped her get situated. She practically fluttered her eyelashes at him.

"It's Ms. Brandt, by the way," I told Rick. "But you don't need to call me that. We were dance partners in tenth grade, after all."

"Oh?" asked Mom.

"Gym class, Mom," I said with a grin. "Square dancing. The only time all year that the boys and girls had gym class together."

"Thank you for that awkward memory," he said, making a face. "Fine, then, Maggie – what would you and your mom like to eat?"

Mom looked overwhelmed by the menu, so I ordered chicken Florentine for her. She always ordered the same thing, so I knew it would please her. I got the Greek pasta with coffee. Rick ordered a steak and fries.

After the waitress left, Rick assumed his best gangster voice and said, "Awright, hand over the goods."

Grinning, I reached into my purse and pulled out the supposed deed. It was looking a little tattered by now – I'd folded it in half to get it in my purse to start with, and the corners had gotten bent and crumpled.

Rick took one look at it and laughed – a big, booming laugh that made heads turn our way. Mom and I exchanged a bewildered glance.

When Rick's laughter would down, he grabbed his napkin and dabbed at his eyes. "I'm sorry," he said. "It's just…" He laughed again. "It's just such a pathetic attempt at a quitclaim deed, that's all. Where did you get this?"

"Sandy brought it over," I said. "He wanted Mom to sign it."

Rick sobered instantly. He read the messy document more carefully, then gave Mom a hard look. "Did he coerce you into signing it?"

"I don't think so," Mom said, distraught. "But…"

Rick transferred his gaze to me. "Tell me what happened."

"I wasn't there for the whole thing," I said, and then described what I'd seen: the deed on the kitchen table in front of Mom, and Sandy hovering over her.

"Did she have a pen?"

"No. And there wasn't one on the table, either."

"And he didn't leave with any papers."

I thought back. "Not unless he had some stuffed in his pocket."

Rick sat back with a sigh. "Well, I think we're safe for now," he said. "For one thing, the clerk won't accept it for filing. It's not in the proper format, and your mother would have needed to have her signature notarized. I presume there was no notary present."

"Not unless Sandy had one stuffed in his pocket along with the signed deed," I said, trying to lighten the mood.

"Probably not, then. Most of them are too big to fit." He smiled. "There's also a form that the state of Indiana requires sellers to file in every real estate transaction. The circuit court clerk wouldn't file a deed without it. My guess is Sandy doesn't know that." He handed the crumpled paper back to me, and I set it to one side of my plate. "I'll stop by the courthouse this afternoon and do a little research, but I'm reasonably certain the house is still yours, Mrs. Muir."

"Thank goodness," Mom said as our food arrived.

"However," he went on as the server put his steak in front of him, "I'd recommend that you make sure your paperwork is in order. Do you have a will?"

"I think so," Mom said.

"I know you do," I said. "You and Dad had them made at the same time. I still have a copy somewhere."

"I'd like to see it, if you can find it," Rick said.

"I'll look for it while I'm packing."

"Oh? You're not leaving Lawrenceburg again, are you?"

Did I detect a note of dismay in his voice? "No, no – I'm staying right here," I said. "I've just been hired at the grocery store as a shift manager, and I'm going to move back in with Mom." I smiled at her. "It'll be easier for both of us."

"I see," he said, with a tight smile. "I wonder..." He paused. "What was Sandy's reason for buying the house from your mother?"

I shook my head. "You got me. He and Diane want to move her to an assisted living facility in Indianapolis. He's got some crazy idea that Mom's not getting optimal care here."

"And why does he think that?"

I felt like I was being put on the spot. "When I left for Rockville in October," I said carefully, "Mom was a little forgetful, but no worse than a lot of older folks. Just normal stuff, you know. But when I got back" – I glanced at her – "she didn't know who I was at first. And I've seen other indications that her memory has gotten worse. Sandy's blaming her problems on the fact that her doctor is Muslim, as if that has anything to do with anything." I swallowed my anger and went on. "And he blames me for leaving her alone. But he had agreed to keep an eye on her – I wouldn't have gone otherwise."

"No need to get defensive," he said mildly. "Everybody needs a break now and then. How long were you gone?"

"About two months. It was only supposed to be a couple of weeks, but..."

He waved off the rest of my sentence. "Doesn't matter. He's her son. You assumed you were leaving her in good hands." He chewed a french fry thoughtfully. "Why did he want the house, though? If he were going to get Medicare to pick up her living costs, I'd put the house in a trust, rather than sell it to a kid. The government will see through that ruse in a minute." He looked at me. "How's he doing, anyway? I haven't seen him in years."

I shrugged. "He's retired, more or less."

Rick laughed shortly. "So am I, more or less. But there's more to my story, and I bet there's more to his, too."

I nodded. "He hurt his back at work a couple of years ago. It's never really healed, and he just couldn't do his job anymore. He's been on disability for about a year – wouldn't you say, Mom?"

"Sure," she said, not really looking up from her meal.

Rick gave me a sympathetic look. I shook my head in resignation. "Anyway, so he's been without a job for about a year. And Diane never worked, that I remember."

"So they're sitting around the house now, getting on each other's nerves. And running short on cash, maybe."

"My daughter Bea suggested the same thing," I said.

"How many kids do you have?" he asked.

"Three. Bea's the eldest – she's a psychologist in Baltimore, and her husband is an internist. They have two adorable children." I couldn't suppress my proud-grandma smile. "Abby, my middle child, is in graduate school in California – something to do with computer software design. And my youngest, Tim, is still finding himself." I let out a little laugh. "He's teaching English as a second language in Mexico right now, assuming he got the problems with his visa straightened out." I made a mental note to call him to find out – and to ask about his girlfriend Ana. "And you?"

"Divorced," he said.

"It's the new adult rite of passage," I said in sympathy.

He blew out a breath. "The marriage went south the same year my father died. That was a tough year." He paused. "We never had children, thank God. But after all that happened, it got so I wondered what I was doing with my life. I made a good living in Indianapolis, but the fun had gone out of it. So I moved back here." He nodded at my mother. "To be closer to my mom as she got older." He looked past me. "She died last year."

"I'm sorry," I said. "Losing a parent is never easy."

"Thanks." He stared at his plate for a moment. Then his head came up. "Anyway, as I was saying, I think your mother needs to update her will, since it sounds like she hasn't done it since your father died. And I would also suggest that she grant someone power of attorney over her affairs – as well as her medical affairs – very soon. Mrs. Muir," he said, "if something happened to you and you needed someone else to make decisions about your finances and your health, who would you want to make those decisions?"

Mom looked up, startled. I wondered whether she hadn't begun to doze off. "What?"

"If you couldn't make decisions for yourself, Mom," I said, "who would you trust to make them for you?"

"You mean about the house?"

"About anything."

"Well, you'll be right here, won't you?"

"Of course," said Rick. "But you need to have a document that states your wishes in that regard, so there's no question about it."

"Sandy wouldn't be happy if I had you make all the decisions," she said. "But you're already doing it."

"Would you rather have Sandy make those decisions for you?" Rick asked.

Mom looked between Rick and me. "No," she said finally. "I want Maggie."

"That's fine," Rick said, as I let out a breath I didn't realize I was holding. "I'd be happy to draw up those papers for you. Now, Mrs. Muir, I have one more recommendation for you."

"Okay," Mom said.

"I think you should put the house in a trust."

"A trust? Why?" I asked.

"Because Sandy may have learned something from this half-hearted attempt at taking the house away from your mom," he said, "and next time, he might be successful."

A chill ran up my back. "Okay. How complicated is it?"

"Not very." He shrugged. "Only the house would be placed in the trust, right? I can structure it so that she has full use and enjoyment of the property until her death. Then, I presume, you and Sandy would inherit it. You two are the only heirs, aren't you?"

"I don't want Diane to get anything," Mom said.

I stared at her. There must have been some bad blood between them that I never knew about. "What if Sandy dies first, though?" I said.

Mom shook her head. "No. Diane gets nothing. That's what my will says now, and that's the way I want to keep it."

"Then that's the way it will be," Rick said. "And your kids would split your share, if you died before your mother. Yes?"

"Yeah, that's fine. Even-steven." I glanced at Mom. "I mean, that's okay with you, right?"

"Of course," she said.

"Okay," Rick said. "That's really all I need to get started. If you can drop your copy of your mother's will by my office – tomorrow morning, say – I can have everything ready for you to sign that afternoon."

"Wow," I said. "You work Christmas Eve?"

"Only for my best clients," he said with a grin. Then he tapped Sandy's makeshift deed with a forefinger. "I think the less time we waste, the better off your mother will be."

Under my blouse, my turtle grew warm against my skin. And I felt a new warmth, too – similar, but slightly different. Sharper. I was sure it meant my new bird agreed with Rick, too.

Chapter 8

Sometimes I can be pretty well organized. Even with half-packed moving boxes stacked everywhere, I managed to find my copy of Mom's will – as well as Dad's, which seemed useless to me. But I stuck both of them in my purse and got back in the car. Maybe Rick would find some value in looking at both wills together. It might give him a sense of what my parents had wanted us to do with their things after they were gone.

His office was downtown, not far from the restaurant where we'd had lunch. I found a parking space nearby, and then just sat in the car for a few minutes, gathering my nerve.

You've gathered by now that Rick and I had a bit of a history. We were part of a group of friends who had hung out together through junior high and high school. Rick had known me when I was Margie, and he knew that I'd changed my name to Maggie because of Rod Stewart's 1970s hit song "Maggie May." And I had known him when he was called Dick and was sick of being called Dickie, and worse, and switched to Rick because it sounded more grown up.

We weren't the only kids from our high school who went to Indiana University – not by a long shot – but we were the only ones from our group who did. Our other friends picked Ball State, Hanover College, and IU's nemesis, Purdue. But Rick and I settled on Indiana, and even put in for housing in the same dorm. It was inevitable that we would cling to one another at first. But by the time I met Gene, in the spring of that year, Rick and I had drifted apart.

Rick had met Gene, of course, and had taken an instant dislike to him. Sometimes, in the years since, I wished I had listened to Rick when he told me Gene was trouble; sometimes I was glad I hadn't, because at least I had gotten the kids – even if their paternal grandmother had made their lives, and mine, miserable.

In my mind's eye, I compared the Rick I remembered from high school with the man I'd had lunch with. He had aged well, I thought. The eyes – a warm brown – were the same; the hair had gone from dark brown to salt-and-pepper, heavy on the salt. He'd put on some weight, but so had I. He had always been a good guy, but now he radiated kindness and competence – maybe even wisdom. And he had appeared to be interested in me at lunch, and it struck me as being more than just professional courtesy. He could have just been catching up with an old pal, too. But he did seem disappointed at the thought that I might leave town.

I wasn't sure whether I was interested in him, or whether the interest I'd perceived in him – if interest it was – had awakened my hormones. I hadn't dated anyone seriously since divorcing Gene; there were slim pickings in my little town, for sure, but I hadn't been in a hurry to look farther afield, either.

Maybe Ruth had primed the pump with her suggestion that I chat up her surgeon, Nathan Stein. He wasn't my type for a number of reasons. But after our disastrous meetup for coffee, I had started thinking about what might constitute my type these days.

The old Rick Hughes might not have fit the bill. This new one, however, seemed to have promise.

I felt a sharp poke in the vicinity of my breastbone. "Ow," I said aloud, rubbing the spot through my shirt – and realized the beak of my bird-on-a-chain was in perfect position to have pecked me there. "Fine," I said, "I'm going. You don't have to tell me twice." I grabbed my purse and the envelope containing my parents' wills and got out of the car.

His office was in a square, modern building just outside of the historic district. I was disappointed; I'd envisioned him in a quirky old Victorian.

I made that my opening salvo when his assistant showed me in. "Why aren't you across the street?" I demanded.

"The rent's cheaper here," he said. "And I can paint my front door any damn color I want." He scooted around the desk to give me a fraternal hug. "How are you, Maggie May?" he asked as he released me.

I smiled brightly and gave him the unvarnished version. "Just great. My mother's memory is shot, my brother's still a jerk, and I'm back working at the same place I worked in high school. And you?"

He winced. "About the same," he admitted, and sank into one of his guest chairs. "It's been hell here. I don't know why I came back, except I felt like I had to, for Mom. And now I don't know why I stay."

"Inertia," I offered.

"Maybe." He stared off into space for a moment. Then he glanced at me. "I knew you were back in town, but I never got around to calling you. I'm sorry."

I shrugged. "There's no need to apologize. I haven't exactly gone looking for anyone from the old gang, either." It was my turn to look away. "You were right about Gene."

"I'm psychic," he said with a goofy grin. Then he got serious again. "What happened there, anyway?"

"You tell me your divorce story, and I'll tell you mine," I said.

He slouched in the chair, ankle on top of opposite knee. "Well, mine is quite predictable. I was working crazy long hours at the firm. She was bored. Started going out clubbing with her friends. One night, she met a guy who didn't work crazy long hours. The night she didn't come home, I called the cops. She read me the riot act for that when she turned up the next morning. She didn't even pretend that she'd stayed over at a girlfriend's house." He rubbed his forehead with his fingertips.

"I'm sorry," I said.

"Anyway, we split and made up two, maybe three more times – and then I was done. Gave her some money and cut her loose. I didn't even have to pay her alimony – she got married again almost as soon as our divorce was final. I hear she's now on husband number three." He shook his head.

"I'm sorry," I said again.

"Your turn," he said with a small smile.

"Well, my story is definitely not predictable," I said, and told him about the intern program that had kept Gene supplied with teenaged girls to screw, and how his parents had covered for him by buying off the girls' parents. "The stress finally got to his father," I said. "He killed himself about a year and a half ago."

"My God."

"In the meantime, my ex-mother-in-law had managed to run off all her kids except Gene. So when she realized she was going to have to have cancer surgery, she insisted that I come out and stay with her. So I did."

His eyes widened. "Just like that?"

"Well, there was a bit more to it. I'd been conditioned for years to let her run roughshod over me." My mouth twisted. "Anyway, it turned out to be a good thing in the end. I discovered why Gene had such a thing for teenage girls. He'd gotten his older sister pregnant, and she'd left town to have the baby and never came back."

Rick sat up. "You think he was secretly in love with her all that time?"

"Maybe. But I think it was more like forbidden fruit. If he couldn't have Debbie, he'd have these other young things instead."

He shook his head. "What a guy. What happened to the child? Do you know?"

"I found him," I said. "He's a trucker. He'd been trying to find his birth parents for years."

"Wow," Rick said, settling back in his chair again. "That's a much better story than mine. Would you like to do investigations for me?"

I laughed. "Thanks for the offer, but I kind of have my hands full at the moment. Oh." I handed him the manila envelope. "Here you go. I found both of my parents' wills."

He peeked in the envelope and tossed it onto his desk. "Thanks. I'll work on the docs for your mother this afternoon."

I eyed him for a minute. "No, really, Rick. What are you doing here in Lawrenceburg?" I gestured around me. "Are you working? Are you retired? Do you wish you were back in Indy?"

"Oh, God, no," he said. "The business of law has changed a lot over the past few decades. It used to be that partners could play golf all day. Now they work harder than the associates." He shook his head. "I guess you could say I'm semi-retired. A lot of what I do is pro bono work. For free," he explained, no doubt noting my expression of confusion. "Like the clinic I did at the senior center this morning. Sometimes a paying customer walks in the door, but I don't charge much because I have investment income and living here is cheap."

Which reminded me – we hadn't discussed payment. "We can pay you," I said tentatively.

He waved it away. "No, no. Your mom qualifies for free legal advice because of her age. I wouldn't dream of taking money from her. Or you."

I wasn't sure how I felt about that, but I nodded. "Thanks, Rick. I know Mom will appreciate anything you can do for her."

"Of course."

It sounded like we were wrapping up, but we both still sat, not moving.

At last, I blurted, "What are you doing for dinner tomorrow?"

"You mean Christmas dinner?" he asked. Then he smiled craftily. "I thought I'd wander over to the Baptist church. They do a nice spread for the poor and the sore at heart, you know."

"Stop it," I said.

"Turkey and cranberries…"

"Rick."

"Mashed potatoes…"

"I mean it!"

"Pumpkin pie for dessert…"

I bent forward and whacked his knee. "Just for that, you're having dinner with us."

He laughed. "No, really, I'll be fine. My aunt and uncle invited me over."

"Come for dessert, then. Gene's sister Abby will be there, and she's bringing her wife and their daughter. You and Abby would get along like a house afire." I grinned archly. "Plus we're having two kinds of pie. *And* real whipped cream."

"You drive a hard bargain, Ms. Muir," he said, and immediately grimaced. "I did it again, didn't I?"

"Yes, you did," I said with mock severity.

"I just can't seem to get used to you being anyone but Maggie Muir." He gave me a sidelong smile that made my stomach flutter.

"Well," I said, stifling a grin, "now that you've messed up my name again, you really do have to come," I said, getting to my feet. "Four o'clock sharp, or we'll eat all the pie without you."

Christmas Day dawned cold but clear. The snow and ice we'd had earlier in the week had all but melted away, but frost crunched underfoot as I loaded side dishes into my car to take them over to Mom's. Between food prep, cooking, and packing, I'd gotten only a few hours of sleep. And I didn't expect this day to be restful. Fun, but not restful.

Mom was still in bed when I got to her place. I let myself in the front door – thankfully, she hadn't locked the screen door before she went to bed – and started getting the turkey ready to go in the oven. I've heard all about how it's not safe to cook stuffing inside your turkey, that you should make it in a separate pan and baby the thing along so it's ready when the bird is ready. Here's what I think: I think people have been roasting various animals with stuffing inside them for thousands of years, probably, and the human race hasn't died out yet. So I stuff my turkey and roast it – and in a regular old oven, too. We don't do any of that goofy giant frying tank business here.

Anyway, the preparations were well underway when Mom finally got up around ten. "Good morning, Sleeping Beauty," I said, mimicking what she used to say to teenaged me when I stayed in bed late on weekends.

She smiled sheepishly. "I heard you out here. I just couldn't seem to wake up. Got any coffee?"

"Right there in the pot," I said, pointing at her ancient coffee maker. I had wanted to get her one of those pod machines like Ruth had for Christmas, but gifts would have to wait 'til I got my first paycheck. "What time did you go to bed, anyway?"

"I don't know," she said.

I paused and looked at her. "Well, what was the last thing you saw on TV?"

"I don't remember," she said, and spilled milk all over the counter instead of into her mug. "Now see what you made me do," she said crossly.

I brandished a dishrag. "All I did was ask when you went to bed," I said. "Here, go sit down. Let me get that for you."

"I can get it myself," she said, glaring, and yanking the dishrag out of my hand. "I'm not a child, you know."

I'd seen that same look on Ruth's face when she complained about the nurse in her doctor's office treating her like a toddler. "Sorry," I said, hoping I sounded contrite.

"You should be," she said, mopping up the milk.

"It's just that I'm just a little concerned about how much you're sleeping, that's all."

"None of your business," she said tartly. "Doesn't concern you."

I shut my mouth and waited until she finished pouring her coffee and took it to the table. Then I slipped into the chair opposite her and said, "Are you upset that I invited Abby and her family to dinner?"

"Abby who?"

"Abby, Gene's sister." I clamped my mouth shut before I could say, *You remember her.*

"He's not coming, too, is he?"

I blinked. "Gene? No, of course not. He's living at Ruth's now."

"Good. I never did like him," she muttered. This was a new side of my mother – opinionated and crabby. I wondered if the dementia was making her angrier, or whether she'd had these thoughts all along and kept them to herself.

"I don't have much use for him these days, either," I said, aiming for levity.

She harrumphed and sipped at her coffee. "Where's Sandy, anyway?"

My gut clenched. "Why? Is he supposed to come today?" *Did you neglect to mention that he called or something?*

"No, he lives here," Mom said. "Doesn't he?"

"Mom," I said. "He lives in Indianapolis. We're home. In Lawrenceburg."

She gave me another of those hard stares, like I was trying to put something over on her.

My heart sank. "You didn't think I was Diane, did you?"

"Of course not," she said. "Haven't you got that bird stuffed yet?"

Chapter 9

Abby, Sallie, and their daughter arrived on Mom's doorstep just after noon. I answered the bell and hugged everybody as they came in, including Sallie and the baby. Abby looked terrific – she'd always been slender, and the southern California sunshine had added reddish highlights to her dark brown hair. And then I remembered she was close to my age, and thought maybe it had all come out of a bottle. If so, I wouldn't criticize her for it; I imagined she had to keep up her appearance in order to get any acting jobs at all in Hollywood.

Sallie was taller than Abby; dark-haired and brown-skinned, she had the sort of bearing that indicated she was used to being in charge. She was taking charge right now of Bernice who seemed lost inside a puffy, quilted bag-like garment with a fur-edged hood. The baby regarded me solemnly as Sallie unzipped her from the thing.

"How was your flight?" I asked. "How is the hotel?"

"Long and fine," Abby said. "We flew into Cincinnati last night, actually. Hi, Mrs. Muir – do you remember me?"

Mom stood tentatively in the kitchen doorway. I stepped in as smoothly as I could. "Mom, this is Gene's sister Abby. And this is her wife Sallie."

Mom's eyes widened, so I'm not sure whether she remembered about Abby or not. In any case, she seemed to take it in stride. "Of course I remember you, Abby. Nice to meet you, Sallie. And who is this?"

"This is Bernice," said Sallie. "Want to hold her?" And she handed off the baby to Mom, who willingly accepted her.

I had a brief flashback to my mother holding each of my children when they were small, rocking and cooing to them as she was doing at that moment with Bernice. I wiped my eye with the back of my wrist and said, "Let me take your coats."

"I'll help," Abby said, and together we hauled the coats, the carseat/carrier, and various bags to Sandy's old room.

"Sallie's wonderful," I offered as we stowed everything on the daybed.

Abby straightened, beaming. "She's pretty terrific. Did I tell you she's a geriatric nurse?"

I blinked. "No, you didn't."

She lowered her voice. "It was her idea that we come to see you this weekend, instead of going to Maryland for Christmas. I was telling her what you said about how much your mom had changed while you were gone, and it concerned her. Usually dementia doesn't come on this fast."

I kept my voice low, too. "See, that's what I thought. Dr. Malik didn't seem too worried about it. But I saw the way Ruth played John so he wouldn't guess how confused she was becoming, and I wondered if Mom wasn't doing the same thing with her doctor."

Abby nodded. "Maybe. Anyway, Sallie will get to the bottom of it. She's amazing." She pronounced "amazing" *uh-MAAAYZ-ing*, as if she were half her age. I couldn't help but smile. "I'm so glad you finally get to meet her. And I'm so glad to *see* you!" She hugged me again. "We need to keep in touch better."

"I'm all for it," I said. Then I stepped back. "But right now, I need to get in some cuddle time with your daughter."

"Sounds great," she said.

Baby Bernice was alert and happy through dinner, but she had a meltdown as we settled ourselves in the living room with our post-dinner coffee. "It's her naptime," Sallie said. "We bought an inflatable crib for traveling. It has its own little air pump and everything. Bernice loves it. Can we put it in your room, Mrs. Muir? That's probably the quietest place in the house."

"Well, um, I guess so," Mom said, starting to lift herself from her chair.

"Oh, no need to get up," Sallie said, patting the shrieking baby's back. "I'll find my way." She exchanged a look with Abby as she passed.

"Poor little puddin'," Abby sighed. "She just gets peopled out sometimes."

"Babies do," I said.

We kept chit-chatting while the air pump did its thing – it was loud enough to hear in the living room, but not ear-splitting. Not long thereafter, the baby wails tapered off. I heard Mom's bedroom door open and close softly, and Sallie emerged from the hallway with a plastic grocery bag in one hand. "I don't think she'll sleep for long," she said.

"I never sleep well in an unfamiliar place, either," Mom said.

"Mrs. Muir, I hope you don't mind," Sallie said, "but I was looking in your medicine cabinet for a safety pin, and I couldn't help but notice these." She set the bag on the coffee table and opened it; several boxes of over-the-counter medicines were inside. "Do you take all of these?"

Mom scooted forward in her chair and looked them over. "Well, yes. This one's for my allergies, and I take this one when I have a cold. And that one is for the acid reflux or whatever they call it on TV. Why?"

"Because Maggie told Abby that your doctor also has you taking Elavil," she said.

Mom nodded. "I've taken it for years. Dr. Malik says it's fine."

"Does he know you're taking all these other drugs, too?"

Mom looked at her in surprise. "Does it matter?"

"Yeah, it does," said Sallie.

"Sallie's a geriatric nurse," Abby put in.

"All of these medications are anticholinergics," Sallie said. "So is Elavil. And the pills you got from the doctor in Indianapolis are anticholinergics, too."

"Why is that a problem?" I asked.

Sallie turned to me. "We all have a chemical in our brains called acetylcholine. It's involved in transmitting signals between our nerves, and it plays an especially big role in cognitive functioning. If we don't have enough of it, our memory suffers."

She gestured at the array of boxes on the table. "All of these drugs lower the level of acetylcholine in the brain. For most adults, it doesn't matter that much – our bodies process the drugs and get rid of them before they can do much damage. But the older we get, the less efficient our bodies are at flushing these things out." She looked at Mom. "They build up in your system over time, and that can affect your memory. The prescription you got from the doctor in Indianapolis was especially dangerous." She looked at me again. "That's probably what tipped her over the edge – taking the Xanax on top of these other drugs."

"Oh," Mom said, her voice small. "Oh, no."

"I bet they're making you sleepy, too," Sallie said.

"She's been sleeping a lot," I said. I looked at the colorful boxes and asked, "What if she stopped taking everything?"

Sallie closed up the bag and tied the handles in a knot. "She should regain cognitive function," she said. "But there's no guarantee that she'd be back to normal." She handed me the bag.

Mom and I looked at each other. "I guess you're going cold turkey," I said.

"I guess I am," she said, a little sadly.

"Don't just quit the Elavil," Sallie said. "Take that bag of drugs with you when you see your doctor next, and talk it over with him. He'll need to taper you off the Elavil, since you've been on it for so long. I'd be happy to talk to him about it, if you like."

"Thanks," I said automatically, as the doorbell sounded.

"Now who could that be?" Mom asked, as I checked my phone for the time.

"Oh, it's Rick," I said, and nearly fell over everyone's feet as I tried to get to the door before he rang the bell again. I didn't want him to be blamed for waking the baby.

He handed me a bottle of wine as he stepped inside. "I didn't want to come empty-handed," he said. "The guy at the liquor store said it would be excellent with pumpkin pie."

"We'll have to try it, then. Come on in." I took his coat and led him the three steps to the living room. "Everyone, this is Rick Hughes. We went to high school together. Rick, this is Abby Brandt-Walters and her wife, Sallie. And of course you know Mom."

"Of course. Hello again, Mrs. Muir," he said, taking her hand briefly. "And it's lovely to meet you ladies. Abby...hmm. You must be Gene's sister. Your facial features are similar."

"That's very kind of you," she said. "Usually I get, 'Gee, you have a big nose – are you Jewish?'" She said it with such a comical twist to her features that we all laughed. "So how do you know Gene?" she asked, looking back and forth between Rick and me.

"They met at IU," I said. "Rick and I hung around together a lot during our freshman year."

"And then Gene cut in ahead of me," Rick said in a mournful tone, "and I never saw Maggie again."

"Stop," I said. "Yes, you did."

Abby watched this interplay with interest. "So what did you think of my brother?" she asked, mischief lighting her eyes.

"I thought he was a jerk," Rick said promptly.

Abby laughed so hard that tears rolled down her face. "So you *have* met him," she managed, before she went off again. Her amusement was infectious; pretty soon we were all laughing along with her.

"What do you do for a living, Rick?" asked Sallie, when the merriment began to wind down.

"As little as possible," he said, which set off another round of giggles. "I'm semi-retired from the practice of law. I have an office in town, but mainly I've been doing pro bono work – advising elderly people who need help with their estates but can't afford a lawyer."

"Rick is drafting a new will for Mom," I said.

Abby turned to my mother. "You're cutting Sandy out of it, I hope."

The idea shocked Mom. "Why ever would I do such a thing?" she asked. "He's my son!"

Abby and Sallie exchanged a glance, but neither one said anything else.

As the silence lengthened, Rick pointed at the bag of pills on the coffee table. "What's with the drugs? Are you planning to open a pharmacy, Mrs. Muir?"

I knew he was trying to change the subject, so I tried to help out. "No, she's applying to help out at the pharmacy," I said with a grin.

But Sallie didn't laugh at my lame joke. Instead, she leveled her gaze at Rick and said, "Tell me. If a client came to you, saying her son made sure she received a prescription that would cause her to develop dementia, what would you advise your client to do?"

Rick looked around the room. "This isn't a hypothetical, is it?"

"No, it's not," Sallie said.

He nodded. "Then I would advise her to adjust her will and grant power-of-attorney to someone she trusts, while she still can." He glanced at Mom. "And further, I would advise her to put her house in a trust."

"Did I tell you about the deed I found?" I asked Abby. When she shook her head, I explained about the handwritten deed that Sandy had left on Mom's kitchen table. "The one thing I can't figure out is what he would gain by it. He says he wants to put Mom in a better situation, but she'd have to be impoverished to convince Medicare to pay for her care. I guess maybe putting the house in his name would accomplish that — but then what? He doesn't plan to live here himself, clearly."

"Maybe he wants to move her in with them, then sell this house and pocket the cash," Abby speculated.

"I'm not moving in with Diane," Mom said. "We spent almost that whole week I was there in the car."

"In the car?" I said. "Going where?"

"Driving around from one house to another," she said. "Sandy said they were looking at houses, but none of the houses where we stopped had 'For Sale' signs out front."

My turtle was vibrating underneath my shirt. I leaned forward to make its movements less noticeable. "So wait. You and Sandy drove to random houses and just went in?"

"*I* never went in," Mom said with a touch of asperity. "Sandy went in. I always sat in the car with Diane. She's a real pistol." Her mouth twisted in disapproval.

"How long were they inside for?" Rick asked.

"Not very long," Mom said. "Just in and out. Then we'd stop in a parking lot and... and..." Her face tightened as if, for once, she was trying not to remember.

"And they would shoot up," Sallie said. She glanced at me. "Heroin. Sandy is buying heroin. Your brother and sister-in-law are junkies."

I shook my head. Sandy, a junkie? The guy who was too straitlaced to try marijuana in the '60s? "I can't believe that. It's too out of character for him."

"Sandy went out on disability," Rick said. "Isn't that what you told me? His doctor probably gave him OxyContin or something similar when he hurt his back, and he just kept renewing the prescription."

"And then he found another doctor when the first one wouldn't prescribe him any more," Sallie said. She turned to me. "This is happening a lot these days. People get hooked on pain pills. Then when they can't get any more from their doctors, they have rebound pain from withdrawal that's so severe that they start buying heroin. Then they overdose."

"But how did Diane get hooked?" I wondered.

"She had a boob job," Mom said. "It was while you were in Maryland."

I frowned. "Wait. Didn't she have a facelift last year?"

Mom nodded. "And a tummy tuck or something, wasn't it, the year before?"

"I wouldn't be surprised," Sallie said. "That's another way people keep the pipeline open. Multiple elective surgeries."

"The hospital was horrible," Mom said, out of the blue.

My gut clenched. "What hospital?" I asked. "When Diane had her boob job?"

"No, of course not. When they overdosed in the car," she said matter-of-factly. "We had been sitting there for a long time. I knew something wasn't right – and besides, I had to pee. So when I saw the police car cruise past, I waved it down." She sounded defensive.

"I bet Sandy got mad at you for it," I said.

"Not him," she said, nose wrinkling as if she'd smelled something rotten. "Diane. That woman has a mouth on her." She shook her head, and then sucked in a breath. "But the ambulance driver said I did the right thing. He said they might not have made it if…" Her voice trailed off.

"Mom," I asked, "did Diane take you to see her doctor before or after this trip to the hospital?"

She paused, frowning. Finally she said, "I don't remember."

Rick looked at me. "I bet that's why Sandy wants this house, Maggie May. He wants to take out a mortgage on it so he can use the money for drugs."

My turtle warmed in assent.

"My God," I said. "No wonder he doesn't want me living here."

Rick reached over to squeeze my forearm, and I gave him a small smile. Then he looked at Sallie and Abby. "How long will you two be here visiting?"

"We fly home Monday," Abby said. "We promised to help Maggie move out of her apartment tomorrow."

"Where are you moving to?" he asked me.

"Here," I said.

A smile spread slowly across his face. "Squatter's rights. I like it. What time are you starting?"

I shrugged. "We hadn't gotten that far in the planning. Why?"

"So I can help, of course," he said. My stomach did an absurd schoolgirl flutter. "I was going to bring the paperwork by tomorrow for your mother to sign, anyway. I was thinking Sallie and Abby might agree to be witnesses."

"Of course," Abby said at once. Sallie nodded.

"The quicker we get this nailed down legally, the better I'll feel," he said.

Just then, we heard a tiny wail from the direction of Mom's bedroom. "I believe that's my cue," Abby said, and got up to tend to her daughter.

"Sounds like it's time for dessert," I said, rising also.

"I'll pour the wine," Rick said as he got up, too, and followed me into the kitchen. "Corkscrew?"

I pointed to the appropriate drawer. "Couldn't find any screw-top bottles, huh?" I teased as I pulled dessert plates from the cupboard.

"The gas station was fresh out," he said, and stuck out his tongue.

"Don't do that unless you intend to use it," I retorted automatically. Then I laughed. "Oh my God. It's been thirty years at least since I used that line on anybody. Sorry. Ow." I rubbed the spot where my bird effigy had just poked me, and went back to slicing pie.

He nodded at my shirt as he poured. "Have you got a party going on in there? I heard something buzzing earlier."

Somewhat embarrassed, I pulled out the chain that my bird and turtle effigies were hung on.

"You still have that turtle?" he said, stepping closer to inspect it. "The bird is new. Well, not *new* new."

I nodded. "I found it the other day, in the woods near where we lived before we moved here."

"Can I touch it?"

I grinned. "You can try."

"What's that supposed to mean?"

"It means they'll let you know if you're not supposed to touch them."

He raised an eyebrow at me, and set down the wine bottle. Then his fingers made contact with the turtle. Nothing happened. I breathed easier.

"I'm still here," he observed. "I guess I passed the test."

"I guess you did."

"Wasn't this thing more tarnished before?"

I had never told Rick the whole story behind the turtle. It just hadn't felt right when we were younger. I wasn't sure whether it felt right now; I needed to trust him implicitly, and I wasn't quite there yet. Besides, we needed to serve dessert. "It was. It's kind of a long story. Grab the whipped cream from the fridge, will you? And here." I took two trays from the top of the fridge and handed him the smaller one. "You can put the wine glasses on this." I placed the bigger tray on the table and loaded plates of pie onto it. Out of the corner of my eye, I watched as he placed the glasses on the tray just so. Then he snatched the dishtowel from the refrigerator door handle and draped it over his arm like a sommelier.

"Very nice," I said. "All you need is a bow tie and tux."

"If only the partners at my old firm could see me now," he said with a rueful sigh. "Ladies first."

I nodded regally and preceded him through the doorway.

Over dessert, we decided to meet at my apartment at nine the next morning. Abby and Sallie had thought to rent a standard-size SUV, and Rick had a pickup – which was a good thing, because it hadn't occurred to me to reserve a truck. "I guess I've been a little preoccupied," I said. "New job, packing, and all this stuff with Mom and Sandy, too."

"It's okay," Abby said. "That's what family is for."

They're not guests, they're family. Ruth had said that once, referring to Riley and my son, Tim. The memory made me smile – and prompted me to say, "What about Rick?"

Abby eyed him up and down. "Close enough," she declared.

He put one hand to his forehead and gestured elaborately as he bowed. "I will endeavor to prove myself worthy of the honor," he intoned.

"Please don't encourage him," I said to Abby.

Rick excused himself shortly thereafter, saying he needed to spend some time at his office, drawing up the documents for Mom. After he left, Abby gave me a sly smile and said, "I think he's a keeper."

I smiled, but rolled my eyes. "He's something. What, I don't know."

She and Sallie left shortly afterward. I joined Mom in the kitchen, where she had begun to clean up. We worked well together, thanks to long years of practice and familiarity with the space. It didn't take long before the leftovers had been stowed in the fridge, the wine glasses had all been hand-washed, and the dishwasher had been started.

I collapsed into a chair at the table. "I like entertaining, but I think I like it better when it's all over."

Mom huffed a sigh as she sat in the other chair. "Me, too. It's nice to see everybody, though." She paused. "Sandy didn't come, huh?"

"Did you ask him?"

"I don't believe I did." She shrugged. "Oh, well. He and Diane probably had dinner with her side."

"Probably. You hungry? Want a turkey sandwich?"

She shook her head. "I'm still full from dinner. Aren't you?"

"I might have room for a little something." I got up and pulled out a loaf of bread.

"You're not having pie, are you?"

I looked at her sideways. "No, Mom. I'm having a sandwich."

"Well, just don't eat all the pie," Mom said. "We need to save a piece for your father."

I stopped. Did we really need to have this conversation again right this second? I looked at my mother; she was sitting in the same chair she always had, wearing the same look she always had when she wanted me to do something kind for Dad or Sandy. And I flashed on the way she had looked the last time I reminded her that Dad was dead. She had crumpled in on herself — as if it had been the first time anyone had told her Dad was gone, and my telling her so matter-of-factly had made the raw wound worse.

I couldn't do that to her again. Not on Christmas.

"Okay," I said, and went on making my sandwich, even though I wasn't hungry anymore.

Chapter 10

My moving crew arrived early. Well, two-thirds of it did. "Bernice was in such a good mood this morning," Abby explained as she, Sallie, and the baby piled in through my front door. "It seemed a shame to waste it. Here." She handed me a coffee in a to-go cup.

"Bless you," I said, yawning. "My coffee maker's packed."

"I called it," Abby said to Sallie. Then she handed off the baby to me. "Let's get moving. Maybe we can get our car loaded before Rick gets here." And the two of them went to work while I played with Bernice.

They had just about filled their SUV when Rick arrived; the three of them then went about packing up his truck. I felt useless. "If someone will take the baby, I'd be happy to pitch in," I said.

"You just stay right there," Sallie said. "You can help unload at the other end."

They took a break around mid-morning. "You don't have as much stuff as I would have thought," Rick said, taking a long pull from the water bottle he'd brought with him.

"Is that a good thing or a bad thing?" I asked.

He shrugged. "It's good in terms of moving. I just expect people our age to have a lot of baggage, I guess. Literally as well as figuratively."

"I left a lot of mine behind in Maryland," I said quietly.

He glanced at Abby and Sallie, who were fussing over the baby. "I'd like to hear about all that sometime," he said, his voice low.

"I'd like to tell you," I said, surprising myself. "But after these guys go home."

"Of course." Then he raised his voice. "Head 'em up, move 'em out," he said. "Maybe we can get everything unloaded by lunchtime."

"Slave driver," Abby groaned.

"I know one thing," Sallie said. "I'm glad our room has a soaking tub. I'm gonna be feeling all this unaccustomed exercise tonight."

I admit that I was worried about how Mom would react to all the excitement – first the holiday meal, and then all these people bringing a bunch of stuff into her house. I'll be honest: I was afraid she would lock the screen door against me, and we'd be stuck. But she welcomed us when we got there. She remembered everyone's names, and she'd even had the presence of mind to move all the throw rugs aside and scoot the furniture out of our path. Best of all, she was happy to take the baby – so the four of us were able to get everything unloaded in a little over an hour.

"Good work, team," said Rick as we flopped down in the living room after the last few things had been brought inside. "Maybe we should hire ourselves out. We could call ourselves the Geezer Movers. What do you think?"

"It needs work," I said. "Seriously, it's hard to believe we're done already. I can't thank you guys enough."

"Just buy us pizza and beer, and we'll be square," Sallie said.

I laughed. "Deal. And I can drive."

"Oh, wait," Rick said. "Before we go, let's get your mother to sign the papers." And he donned his coat again and went out to the car to get them, pulling out his phone as he strode down the steps.

"Seriously, Maggie," Abby said. "He's a keeper." She and Sallie nodded emphatically.

"Noted," I said, as I watched Rick through the picture window. I was falling, but I didn't want to fall all the way – not yet. It just seemed too good to be true. I kept waiting for the other shoe to drop.

Mom came down the hallway to the living room, carrying a sleeping baby. "Are you done?" she asked.

"Oh, here, let me take her," Abby said, springing up from the couch.

"She's no bother," Mom said, smiling, but she let Abby have Bernice all the same.

"Rick's getting the papers for you to sign," I said. As I spoke, a car pulled up to the curb, and a woman carrying a leather satchel hopped out.

Rick waved at her, and then followed her up the steps as the car drove away.

"Mrs. Muir, this is Marie," he said. "She's going to notarize your signature."

She eyed the two of them suspiciously. "On what?"

"On the papers Rick made out for you," I said.

She turned her glare on me. "What papers? This isn't that foolishness about giving the house to Sandy, is it?"

"No, ma'am," Rick said. "This is going to keep the house away from him."

She still looked dubious. But Rick was patient with her. He sat down at the kitchen table with us and went page by page, explaining every item in each document and confirming that everything was set up exactly the way she wanted it to be.

"Diane can't get anything, can she?" Mom asked, more than once.

"No, Mrs. Muir," Rick responded each time.

"Good," Mom said. "That's the way I want it."

I wondered again what my sister-in-law had done to her in years past – but with Mom's memory the way it was, I didn't know if I would ever find out.

There weren't enough chairs to go around, but I was content to lean against the sink and watch as everybody took turns signing each piece of paper. At last, it was done; Marie crimped the final piece of paper with her embosser and handed everything to Rick.

"Thanks, everybody," he said, sliding the papers back into his attaché case. "I need to run and get these copied so I can file the deed with the clerk on Monday."

"What about lunch?" I asked.

"Sorry," he said with a smile. "I'll have to take a rain check. We need to have our ducks in a row before Sandy makes another move. Abby, Sallie, it's been great to meet you. You'll still be around tomorrow, won't you?"

"Sure," Abby said. "Our flight isn't until Monday."

"Great. I'll bring the copies by. I'd like to give you two a courtesy copy for safekeeping. I've found, in cases like these, that it's better to have as many copies distributed with disinterested parties as possible." He shook hands with Mom. "Always a pleasure to see you, Mrs. Muir."

"You too," Mom said.

He turned to me. "Sorry," he said again.

I sucked up my disappointment and cocked my head at him. "You know this means I'm treating you to pizza another day, right? You're not getting out of this."

"I'm counting on it," he said. He stood for another moment, uncertain. Then he slipped an arm around my shoulders and pulled me to his side.

My arms went around his waist. "Thanks for all of this," I said quietly.

"Happy to help," he said, and released me. "See you tomorrow." Then he followed Marie out the door. She hopped into his truck on the passenger side, and they roared away.

"I guess he's dropping her somewhere," Sallie said, coming to stand next to me with the baby propped on one shoulder.

"I'm sure that's it," I said, beating back the green-eyed specter that wanted to consume me. *They're professional acquaintances, for God's sake. He didn't even touch her.* But no matter what my rational mind said, another part of me wanted to be in the car with him.

I forced myself to turn away from the window. "Let's order the pizza. I'm starving."

Partway through our late lunch, Bernice began to get fussy again. "We should probably go," Sallie said, as the baby's mewling ramped up; a full-bore howl wasn't far off.

"We should," said Abby, getting up from the table. "Sorry to eat and run, but…"

"You take that child home and put her down for a nap," Mom said, shaking her finger at them.

"That's exactly what we're going to do," said Abby with a grin. Sallie was already encasing Bernice in her quilted baggie. "Thanks for everything."

"No, thank *you*," I said. "I'd still be hauling boxes if you guys hadn't all pitched in." Hugs were exchanged all round, and they managed to make their escape before the Great Wailing erupted.

Then I left Mom to her own devices and went to my room to begin unpacking. Not everything from my one-bedroom apartment would fit in my childhood bedroom, obviously; I was going to have to store a lot of boxes in the attic. Right now, they were stacked in Sandy's old room, out of the way. I planned to put them upstairs later, after I made sure everything I needed was in the boxes that we'd put in my room – and after I got some rest.

The first thing I did was to clear a few things off the nightstand on the far side of my childhood bed – the one no one could see from the hallway. There, I set up the candle, and my basket of feathers and rocks and things. I lit the candle. And then I took the chain from around my neck and placed my turtle and bird effigies in their new home.

They looked much as they had on the day when I found the bird – or rather, the day the bird found me. No more tarnish had magically melted away from either one of them, but then neither had accumulated any more, either.

Still, I felt like I hadn't made much progress. When I had first met Granny, she'd gone into a sort of trance and told me that three doors would close on me, and I would close three more, before the right door opened for me. While I was in Rockville, I had heard two doors close in my head. The first one shut when I declared I didn't want to work for anyone who couldn't understand that there was more to life than making money. The second one closed at the end of that disastrous date I had with Ruth's surgeon. So I still had four to go – including, I thought, all three of the doors that would close against me.

I wondered what that would be like. I had a feeling it wouldn't be pleasant.

It didn't help that I felt like I was spinning my wheels here in Lawrenceburg. No, actually, it felt like I was losing ground. Here I was, at the age of fifty-eight, giving up my own apartment and moving back into my childhood bedroom. I had a management job at the same grocery store where I'd worked when I was in high school – and it had not escaped my notice that I was the oldest shift manager on the staff. The rest were all in their late twenties or early thirties.

I knew in my heart that I was right where I needed to be: here in my hometown, helping Mom navigate her old age. Padding the corners for her, as she had done for me when I was small. But it didn't make me feel any less a failure.

And I missed my kids. I missed Bea and John and their adorable youngsters – four-year-old Royce, who called me Nokomtha, and Ryker, who at eighteen months wasn't entirely convinced I was okay. The only way to convince him would be regular, face-to-face contact, which I could hardly manage from five hundred miles away.

I missed Tim, too, even though I should have still been mad at him. He had expended great effort over the past few years to convince me he was unreachable. As it turned out, he had a valid reason to avoid me: he believed I had left him with his father because I didn't love him. We had just begun to patch things up when he was called away. I ached to cement that beginning, and make more progress. But he was in Mexico City, tending to his girlfriend, and I had no idea when I'd see him again.

I missed my middle daughter Emily. I hadn't seen her in quite some time; she was in grad school in California, and she too was good at coming up with excuses to avoid coming home. I thought I might invite her here for New Year's. Why, we could have all of them here for New Year's. Mom would love Bea's kids, and it would be so good to have everyone I loved under the same roof again.

Neither the turtle nor the bird reacted to my brilliant plan.

Sighing, I cast a look at the stacks of boxes crowded around the bed. Then I blew out the candle, kicked off my shoes, and lay back to rest my eyes, as Mom sometimes called it.

Moments later, I was dreaming.

I glided silently along, as near as I could get to the riverbank without going aground, looking for opportunity.

Frustration was my constant companion. I was sick and my mate was sick, and nothing I did made any difference. I knew what was causing our problems, but it was also the only thing that eased my pain. Now we were on the verge of being turned out of our home. I needed a break – badly.

Then I saw the doe.

She had a thing I needed. I'd been watching her for some time now – watching and waiting for a chance to snatch this thing. Then her guardian had delivered her into my power! The first step had been taken, and it was working; she seemed hesitant, almost dazed. Perhaps now was the time.

A tiny voice in my head gasped. "The doe has given you so much, yet you would treat her this way? Have you no humanity left in you? Have you no shame?"

I smacked the voice into silence with a single swipe of my ebony paw. I had no patience for melodrama – not with my wife so ill, our lives so shattered. Not with the sickness demanding to be fed.

I changed course, angling toward the far bank.

Out of nowhere, a turtle sped toward me. It moved so purposefully, so fast, that I swerved to avoid it. Still, it came on. The thing had a death wish! Well, I was happy to help it achieve its goal.

I played with the thing, batting it about, allowing it to think it had a chance of besting me – me, an Underwater Panther, being beaten by a turtle! At last, I tired of the game. Seizing it in my front paws, I held it to my mouth and bit down hard.

One of my upper canines shattered on the iron plates of its back. Howling in pain, I threw the thing as far as I could, and swam away.

Then I cursed my stupidity. I'd forgotten about the doe! The turtle would be long gone by now. I could double back and…

Something white-hot swept past my head, so close that my ear tufts crisped and blew away on the fiery wind.

I shot up out of the water, coming to my full height, and roared in pain and indignity. "Who are you, that you would dare to attack Mishepeshu? Show yourself!"

A trill of birdsong answered me. I turned toward the sound — and there, in the crook of a tree, I saw my nemesis. "Thunderbird!" I growled, for it was she. "Why must you always interfere with my plans?"

The bird was a fraction of my size, yet she addressed me as her equal — for she was, as I had learned over and over again. "Begone, Mishepeshu," she warbled. "Leave the doe alone. She is under my protection now."

"Under your..." I stopped in sudden understanding. The doe's guardian had returned, with reinforcements. I would have to be craftier if I were to reach my goal.

"Don't try it," Thunderbird warned, ruffling her fiery feathers to make herself look bigger. Thunder rumbled.

"Don't threaten me," I replied.

"It's not a threat," said Thunderbird. "Go home to your mate. And see to that broken tooth. You're bleeding in the water. Something might decide to attack you while you're wounded."

With a roar, I dove deep and swam away. But it was not over. It would never be over.

I woke with a start and sat up. Golden shadows danced on the walls, as if the room were on fire. At first, I thought I hadn't quite doused the candle flame and it had flared up again while I slept. But no, the candle was out. It was my bird effigy lighting up the place – glowing erratically, as if licked by ethereal flames.

I rolled off the bed and crouched before the effigy, awestruck. I heard a single word in my head:

BEWARE.

Then the light went out.

I dropped to a seat on the floor with some difficulty – I was wedged in between the bed and a stack of boxes – and waited for any further messages, or a renewal of the light show. But both the turtle and the bird were quiet again.

"I was pretty sure I was wary before," I said at last. I stuck an elbow on the edge of the mattress and levered myself to my feet. "But I will do my best to be extra vigilant from now on. I'll need your help, though."

It seemed the tarnish on the bird receded a little bit.

"Thanks," I said, and sat on the edge of the bed to think.

I'd had a number of dreams and visions since beginning this adventure. Most of them had been troubling in some way, and a couple had left me an emotional wreck. But this was the first time I'd had a dream in which I was clearly inside someone else's head.

I'd dreamed that I was a water panther once before, and I had perceived it as an indication that there was a dark side to my emotional makeup that I didn't always allow out into the light. The sense I had was that I needed to integrate that dark side – my shadow self – into the personality that I typically showed the world. Granny had charged me with renewing the earth, after all, and I presumed I would need every tool in my arsenal, both light and dark, to accomplish that. I could not allow the bad stuff to blindside me. Moreover, I suspected, in order to get the job done I was sometimes going to have to be a jerk.

But the dream I'd just had was of a different sort. I recognized the story, of course. It was the same dream I'd had recently, but from Sandy's point of view. I remembered feeling his frustration, his concern for his mate, and his anger at the turtle who stood in the way of getting at the doe. He clearly knew the doe was Mom; however, he did not appear to realize that I was the turtle. I wondered for a moment how the water panther would envision Mom's guardian in this allegorical setting, but nothing came to me.

Thunderbird, however, was clearly an old acquaintance of the water panther's. I glanced at the bird effigy again. I'd thought it was a falcon at first, or maybe a hawk. But apparently not.

I got up and shifted a few boxes around until I found the one with my tablet in it. Then I plopped back on the bed and did a little research. The Shawnee, like many other Native American tribes, believed thunderstorms were the result of a battle between Thunderbird and an underwater monster; the Shawnee had called their critter Mishepeshu. Of course, my effigies were from an earlier civilization, but I'd caught glimpses of a connection between the mysterious, vanished Hopewell Indians and the Shawnee. In the Southwest, I knew from my anthropology courses, experts had speculated for years about what had happened to the Anasazi, the culture that built the fabulous cliff dwellings at Mesa Verde. They seemed to have vanished without a trace – until somebody finally thought to ask the Hopi. It turned out the Anasazi were their ancestors.

Maybe that's not quite how it happened, but that's the gist of it. And my gut was telling me the Hopewell and the Shawnee were related in a similar way.

As interesting as that line of thought was to pursue, it didn't have a lot of bearing on my current dilemma. The dream – assuming it really was of mystical origin, and not just my subconscious piecing things together to fit my preconceptions – confirmed that Sandy had no compunction about hurting Mom to get what he thought he needed from her. He was prepared to turn our mother – and me – out of this house so he could feed his addiction.

As if I'd needed any confirmation after what Mom had said about his and Diane's drug abuse.

Goodness knew what he planned to do with Mom. Maybe he and Diane really did intend to find a senior housing complex in Indianapolis where they could park her on the government's dime. Or maybe they intended to move her in with them, skiffling her Social Security check and whatever other retirement funds she had, and keeping her loopy so she wouldn't question what was going on.

It was a lot to take in. This was my brother we were talking about. It didn't matter whether the drugs were turning him amoral or encouraging a tendency he'd had all along. I was supposed to be on his side – wasn't I? Mom had always told us to be nice to one another. And siblings are supposed to stick together, aren't they? They're supposed to help one another, aren't they?

Maybe. Maybe not. Sandy had made his opinion of my lifestyle abundantly clear: I needed to grow up already and get out, and he was not going to help me do it.

No, my loyalties lay with Mom. I needed to keep going to bat for her and protecting her from him. I needed to protect myself from him, too. And if I had to be a jerk to do it, well, then, that's what I would do.

My turtle lit up with a soft, red-gold glow, and a little more of the tarnish disappeared.

Chapter 11

Abby called me the following morning. "Get dressed and meet us at Epic Buffet in fifteen minutes!" she said. "We're not taking no for an answer. The reservation is already made."

"What on earth...?" I said

"Sallie and I went to the casino last night. We, uh, figured you wouldn't be interested in coming."

"Not really, no," I said.

"So anyway," she went on, "we took turns holding the baby and playing the machines – and we won!"

"Congratulations," I said.

"It's not a lot, but it's enough to buy brunch for the three of us."

"Oh no," I said. "You don't want to blow your winnings on me. You should save them for a rainy day. Put them in a college savings account for Bernice or something."

While I voiced my objections, Abby passed the phone to Sallie. "Don't try to talk us out of it, Maggie," she said. "This is what we want to do. You deserve some time that's responsibility-free – not just because of what you've been through so far with your mother, but because it's not going to get any easier."

I could hear Abby taking the phone back. "And don't forget all the stuff with my mom, too."

"How could I possibly forget?" I said. "You're right. It's been a crazy few months." And I'd been in charge of a lot of stuff over those few months. "A break would be wonderful – even if it's only brunch."

"Good. That's settled. We'll see you in a few."

I had no sooner hung up from talking to them than my phone rang again. "Nothing like being popular," I muttered as I answered it.

"Hello, Maggie May," Rick said. "I was hoping to catch you in."

My stomach did a little leap; I rolled my eyes at it. "What did I use to call you in high school?" I asked.

"I don't recall that you had a pet name for me."

"Pet name," I scoffed. "Right. I was thinking more along the lines of a nickname."

"Why?"

"I just can't believe I didn't retaliate when you called me Maggie May."

"Hey, you *liked* it in 1973." I could hear the smile in his voice.

"I don't mind it all that much now," I admitted. "I just feel the need for ammunition, that's all. Hmm. What about Little Ricky?"

"No," was all he said.

"You never went by Ricky. Why is that?"

"Because I hated it."

"Did you? Why?"

"Because of Ricky Ricardo," he said.

"Oh, right! Lucille Ball's Cuban husband. Now I remember. You said some stupid kid in third grade started babbling in fake Spanish whenever he saw you."

"*He* was in third grade. I was in second. And thanks for reminding me of that charming memory."

I ignored his complaint. "That was before I knew you," I said softly. "Doesn't that seem odd? Seems like I've known you my whole life."

He was silent for a moment – long enough that I wondered whether I had said something wrong. Then he cleared his throat. "Anyway, the reason I was calling was to tell you that I dropped the deed into the after-hours box at the clerk's office yesterday. It'll be filed first thing Monday morning. Your mother doesn't have to worry about her house falling into the wrong hands any more."

"Good news," I said, using my professional voice. "She'll be very pleased."

"I'd like to stop by sometime today and drop off the copies," he said. "When would be a good time?"

"I'm meeting Abby and Sallie for breakfast in a few minutes," I said. I nearly added, *Want to join us?* But I felt funny about asking them whether I could bring someone. So instead, I said, "We should be done by noon. Why don't you come over then?"

"Noon it is," he said.

Breakfast was just the break I needed. The baby behaved herself, and my former sister-in-law did not. We alternated between howling with laughter and dissolving into giggles. But no one else in the restaurant seemed to mind. Abby, with her theatrical background, turned heads in a good way, and Sallie exuded an air of grace.

That left me the role of the frumpy friend, but I was okay with it. "It's my job to make you two look even more fabulous by comparison," I said.

"Oh, cut it out. You're beautiful in your own way," said Abby. "Rick doesn't seem to have a problem with how you look."

I gave them both my best mysterious smile and ducked my head toward my plate.

We made it back to Mom's well before noon – which, it turned out, was a good thing. "Whose car is that in your spot in the driveway?" Sallie asked, after we'd parked at the curb.

"My brother's," I said, mentally girding my loins. "Come on."

One look told the story: Mom, wearing a stubborn expression, sat at the kitchen table. Sandy leaned over her, much as he had before, with one hand on the back of her chair and the other braced on the edge of the table.

But this time, Diane had come along for the ride. Clearly, she was the lookout, because she popped up from the living room couch as soon as we walked in and said, "Sorry, you can't go in there."

"I can go anywhere I please in this house," I said, striding up to her. "I live here." She was taller than me by a few inches, thanks to her wedge-heeled boots, but I was broader. She looked pale and drawn – a look I was beginning to associate with drug abusers.

"Yeah, I saw all your crap in my room," Sandy yelled. "Didn't I tell you you weren't welcome here? You need to get that junk out of there right now, or I'll toss it out by the curb."

"You and what army?" Abby said, stepping around Diane and me to stand in the kitchen doorway, arms akimbo.

"Who the hell are you?" Sandy demanded.

"Watch your language, mister," Mom said, glaring up at him. "There are ladies present."

He laughed. "Where?"

Mom opened her mouth to reply, but thought better of it.

He turned to me. "Tell your girlfriends to go home, Maggie. This is a family matter."

"We *are* family, you dolt," Abby said.

I pushed past Diane and joined Abby at the door. "Sandy, you remember my sister-in-law Abby," I said.

"She's no family of mine," he said. "She's not even family of yours any more."

"What exactly are you doing here?" I said. Then I spied a fresh crop of papers sitting in front of Mom. I couldn't help myself – I laughed. "Oh, no. You're not going to try to get her to sign another bogus deed, are you?"

He bristled. "It's an actual legal document, valid in the state of Indiana," he said. "It said so on the internet."

"Because everything on the internet is true," I said. "Right. Did you actually use a word processor to fill in the blanks this time, or did you hand-write stuff in again?"

Bernice chose that moment to begin to cry. Sallie, who still stood by the door, rocked her in her arms.

"Whose baby is that?" Sandy demanded.

"Mine," said Abby. "And the woman holding her is my wife."

"You're *dykes*?" Sandy said. "Mom, your sweet baby girl brought *dykes* into this house! What happened to your morals?"

"My morals have always welcomed anyone in this house," Mom said, pushing her chair back.

Someone knocked on the front door. Sallie braced Bernice on one shoulder and bent forward to open it.

At the same time, Sandy looked at me. "Maybe she's a dyke, too," he said with a sly smile. "Are you, Maggie? Maybe that's why you haven't ever gotten married again, huh?"

"Well, hello, everyone," Rick said from the threshold. "I guess I didn't miss the party, after all. Sandy, Diane, nice to see you again." He strode forward, wrapped one arm around my shoulders, and planted a kiss on my lips. It lasted quite a while.

I couldn't have been more surprised if he'd danced the tango with a rose in his teeth.

When Rick broke it off at last, he hugged me to his side and said evenly to Sandy, "She's not gay."

My brother harrumphed. He straightened with a wince, then crossed his arms. "Why, it's Baby Huey," he said. "What are you doing, sniffing around here?"

Trust my brother the jerk to remember the disparaging nickname the kids had had for Rick. I'd blocked it out.

"As it happens," said Rick, letting go of me to fiddle with the catch on his attaché case, "Baby Huey grew up to be Richard Hughes, attorney at law. Ah, here we go." He extracted a manila folder and began passing around the papers inside it. "One for Abby and Sallie, one for Maggie, one for Mrs. Muir – and a courtesy copy for you." He handed the final copy to my brother. "An original is already filed with the county clerk, and I have another one in the safe in my office."

Sandy glanced over it suspiciously. "What's this for?"

"Well, in essence," said Rick, "your mother's house is now held in trust. No one can take it away from her – not you or anybody else. And that's the way it will stay, until either she dies or the house is destroyed."

"You can't do that!" Sandy yelled. "What gives you the right?"

"*I* gave him the right," Mom said, getting to her feet.

"You don't know what you're saying, Mom," Sandy said, beginning to wheedle. "You've had some hard times here lately, what with Maggie deserting you and all."

"She didn't desert me," Mom snapped. "The only mistake *she* made was thinking you and Diane could be trusted to look in on me!"

"But Mom," he said, "your memory is going…"

"My memory is not so bad that I don't remember the two of you in the E.R., recovering from your drug overdose," she said.

Sandy shut his mouth, and his look warned her to do the same.

I used the sudden silence to address both him and Diane. "You two have a serious problem, and I truly hope you can find the courage to get treatment for it. But I am not going to stand by and let your problem become Mom's problem – or mine." I could feel both turtle and bird buzzing under my shirt.

"Among the papers I just handed you," Rick said, "you'll find a copy of the power-of-attorney documents that I drew up for your sister. If at any time in the future, your mother becomes incapacitated, Maggie will be in charge of making all legal and medical decisions for her."

"Goddammit!" Sandy roared.

"I *told* you this wouldn't work," Diane said to him. "I told you we'd never get away with it. God, you're such a *screw-up*."

"Shut up!" he yelled. He glared at everyone, then snatched his coat from the back of the couch and grabbed Diane by the wrist. "Come on. Let's go."

"You're hurting me," she complained, but didn't try to break away.

He turned at the doorway and said, "This can't be legal." He shook the fist that held the papers. "Enjoy your victory, little sister, because it won't last." Then he banged out the front door, dragging his wife after him.

Miraculously, Bernice had calmed down while all the drama was going on, but she began wailing again when Sandy slammed the door. Sallie went back to shushing and rocking her.

Over Bernice's cries, I heard Sandy's SUV roar to life and speed away. I went to Mom and hugged her. "Don't worry," I told her. "He can't turn us out."

"I'm not worried," she said. "I just wish I knew how I'd managed to raise such an awful man." She sniffed and lay her head against my shoulder. "He was such a nice boy."

Maybe to you, he was. I didn't say it aloud, though. If she wanted to persist in believing that Sandy was a decent guy once, I'd let her.

"It's the drugs talking," Abby said.

"Of course it is," I said. Then I looked at Rick. "That was nicely played. Thanks for being the cavalry."

"Just another service we provide," he said with a lopsided grin.

Bernice was running out of steam, but so was Sallie. "We should go," she said quietly to Abby.

Abby glanced at the wall clock above the sink. "We should," she said. "Maggie, it was lovely to see you. Be sure to call again when you've got more family drama – it's better than watching a movie."

I laughed and hugged her, then hugged Sallie and the baby, and saw them both out. Then, with a big sigh, I flopped down on the couch.

"Your memory seems better," Rick said to Mom as he took a seat near me.

Mom eased into her favorite chair. "It does, doesn't it? Maybe Sallie was right about all those extra pills I was taking."

"I'm sure she was," I said, pushing myself to a more ladylike, seated posture. I was relieved that Mom seemed to be getting her memory back, but I wished I could forget that Zed had said the improvement wouldn't last. I looked over at Rick. "What are you doing for dinner tonight? I still owe you a pizza."

"And beer," he said.

"And beer." I grinned.

His own smile faded. "I think I need to take another raincheck."

"Oh, come on!" I said. "I'm not *that* bad a kisser."

He blushed. "Sorry about that. I couldn't think of anything else to do."

"Was I complaining?" I arched an eyebrow at him.

Mom looked at each of us in turn. Then she said, "Excuse me," got up, and headed down the hall to the bathroom.

I hooked at thumb at her retreating back. "She's always been quick on the uptake."

"She has. And that wasn't nearly as good a thing when we were in high school," he said. "Look, Maggie. I don't know what's going on here. I thought I was helping out an old friend and her mother, and suddenly…" He fell silent for a moment. "Maybe we're going too fast," he added.

"Too fast? I squeaked. "It's. Just. Pizza."

"Yeah, I know. It's just…"

"Pizza," I said again. "And beer." Then I had to add, "Is it the booze that worries you? Will you say yes if I promise to keep my hands to myself?"

He shook his head. "I don't know how to respond to that. I can't tell which answer will get me in less trouble."

"Rick," I said.

"Okay, here's a practical response. I'm not sure you should leave your mom alone tonight. The weasel could double back."

My turtle rattled in agreement.

"Seriously, though," I said, "what can he do?"

He shrugged. "Legally? Not much. If he had a lawyer, he could try to contest the validity of the documents by saying your mother wasn't in her right mind when she signed them. But she hasn't been declared incompetent, and that would weigh against him." He balanced an ankle on his opposite knee. "Besides, legal advice typically costs money, and we know he doesn't have any. If he did, he wouldn't be trying so hard to steal the house. No, I'm not worried about a legal challenge."

"What, then?"

He tented his fingers and tapped his forefingers against his lips. "How do I put this?" he said. "Sandy's desperate. Desperate people have been known to do things they wouldn't otherwise consider."

"Violent things," I said. The hairs on my forearms stood up when I said it.

"Exactly. You may want to alert the police."

I raised my hands, palms up. "And what will they do? We don't have a restraining order against him, and it wouldn't do much good if we did. He'd just ignore it."

"Yeah, those things are pretty ineffective," he admitted. "If he were the sort of person who respected the law, you wouldn't need the restraining order in the first place. But at least the authorities would know there's the potential of violence. They might increase patrols around the neighborhood."

I thought of Mom's neighbors wondering why there were more cops around, and how embarrassed she would be if they figured out it was because of us. "I can call them tomorrow," I said, dubious. "But I think it might make things worse if he does come back."

"Up to you," he said.

"Now," I said, "About dinner. I don't have to work tomorrow, so let's do dinner tomorrow night."

"You drive a hard bargain, Maggie May," he said. "All right, fine."

"Fine," I echoed, sealing the deal. Then I cupped one hand to the side of my mouth and called, "Okay, Mom. You can come back out now."

It wasn't until after Rick left that I began to shake.

One of the reasons I'd pushed so hard for more time with Rick that night was that Sandy's threats had unnerved me. I believed Rick when he said there was nothing Sandy could do to challenge the trust and the power-of-attorney document. But there was no doubt in my mind that he would throw my stuff in the gutter, given half a chance, and I was convinced the cops wouldn't care in the least.

"If you're cold, go put on a sweater," Mom said. We were sitting in the living room with the TV on. She was watching some police procedural; I was mostly there to keep her keep her company.

"I'm not cold."

"You're shivering," she pointed out.

"I'm not…" And I stopped. There didn't seem to be any point in denying it. "I'm fine, Mom, really." But I pulled the crocheted afghan off the back of the couch, wrapped up in it, and went back to my doleful ruminations.

I wasn't worried about my ability to take care of myself, and I certainly didn't believe I needed a man to protect me. What worried me was what Sandy might do to Mom while he was trying to throw me out of the house. I kept flashing on that first dream, when Turtle Me had ended up stranded on my back, and Mom had flipped me over with her nose. I was sure she would try to protect me in real life, too, and I couldn't predict what Sandy would do if she got in his way. He'd already proven that he was willing to make her crazy. It seemed a short step from there to physical harm.

Something sharp poked my breastbone. "Ow," I said automatically. Then, realizing what had happened, I said to the thunderbird, "Cut it out."

Mom's head swiveled in my direction. "Maggie, are you okay?"

I sighed. "No. Sorry. It's been a long day. I'm going to head for bed."

"All right. See you in the morning."

I folded the afghan and put it back. Then I kissed Mom on top of her head, and she patted my arm awkwardly. "Everything's going to be okay," she said. "You'll see."

I did my best to smile, but I don't think I convinced her that I believed her any more than I could convince myself.

Chapter 12

The following day, I puttered around the house – I did my laundry and Mom's, unpacked some boxes, and otherwise filled the hours when I would see Rick again. I wasn't sure why, after all the years of just being friends, I was suddenly so excited about going out with him. Maybe we had both needed to get to the right place in life? Or maybe we were the other's only likely suspect for miles around?

I fantasized for a few moments about us being the subjects of one of those newspaper feature stories about adorable couples: "Friends Forever, Lovers at Last" might be a good headline. It had alliteration going for it, but I wasn't sure the local paper would publish a story with "lovers" in a headline where little kids could see it. Not that kids ever read the newspaper these days, but they might come across it on the internet – where they could easily find worse things than the word "lovers."

I knew I was jumping the gun; after a few dates, we might well discover that we were less compatible now than we'd been in college. But the fantasy kept my mind off the question of Sandy – and Rick's advice that I call the cops on him.

At last, I ran out of things to do. I wandered the house, and stopped in the doorway to Sandy's old room. Those ten or twelve boxes I intended to shove up into the attic were still sitting there, and I debated whether I had the energy to do it. Most of the boxes contained household items like my pots and dishes, which I didn't need now but might at some future date when I lived alone again. But one box contained mementos from when my kids were babies: tiny booties, locks of impossibly fine hair, and, in Bea's case, a baby book I'd used to document her first year. I'd meant to make baby books for Emmy and Tim, too, but I'd never gotten around to it.

I thought of grabbing that box and stowing it in my room – it seemed vulnerable to me, sitting in what increasingly felt like hostile territory. But it was on the bottom of a stack, and I didn't feel like shifting boxes to get to it just then. In fact, the thought of pulling down the ladder and manhandling those boxes into the attic made me tired.

With one last look at the box of baby things, I turned away and went back into my own room. I straightened the duvet on the bed, and used a tissue to rub at a forty-year-old spot on the mirror. It didn't come off this time, either. At last, I had to admit to myself that I needed to just call the police and get it over with.

I settled myself on the living room couch and picked up the phone.

The dispatcher I talked with was sympathetic, but not very helpful. Her hands were pretty much tied. Absent a restraining order or an imminent threat, there wasn't much the police could do to keep Mom and me safer than we already were. The dispatcher offered to have an officer stop by to talk to us about keeping our property safe: keeping the doors and windows locked, staying alert for trouble when we left home, and that sort of thing. I declined. Mom had been beating all that advice into my head for fifty years. But I thanked the dispatcher for her help anyway.

As I hung up, I had tears in my eyes. The cavalry wasn't coming. If my brother tried anything, I was going to have to be the one to stop him.

The pizza place we had all loved back in high school was still around, but Rick had suggested a different restaurant for dinner: wood paneling and leather-topped tables instead of football jerseys and Formica, and "flavors to please a more mature palate," as he put it.

"That's funny," I said as I perused the menu. "I don't see any old-fart food here."

He eyed me. "Define old-fart food."

"You know. Oatmeal. Prunes."

He kicked me under the table. "I meant the pizza toppings."

"Oh," I said, and gave him a sly grin. He was right, of course; the list of toppings included things like sun-dried tomatoes and artichoke hearts. "This seems a little trendy for Lawrenceburg."

"You'd be surprised at how cosmopolitan we are hereabouts," he said, putting on a bit of a southern twang. "We get your cable television and everything."

"Uh-huh."

The waitress came by and we gave her our order. As she moved away, Rick asked in a normal voice, "How's your mother doing?"

"Fine," I said. "You were right – her memory is gradually getting better. She hasn't called me Margie in a couple of days."

"Sounds encouraging." He paused. "Did you call the police about…?"

I put down the menu. "I did, and they weren't much help. Without a restraining order, there's nothing they can do. And of course we can't get a restraining order unless he's been violent."

"There are a couple of other actions that would qualify," he said. "But you're right – he hasn't crossed that line yet." He put his own menu down. "This must be hell for you."

"It's not a lot of fun," I said. "But I feel better that I'm living in the house now, instead of several miles away. It'll be easier to keep an eye on everything. Including Mom." I picked up the menu again, but didn't really look at it. "I feel like this is where I need to be at this point in my life."

"And what happens when this point in your life is over?"

I looked at him. "What do you mean?"

He raised his hands. "Well, at some point your mother won't need you any more. Either she'll be too ill for you to take care of her at home, or she will have passed on. What will you do then?"

I gave a short laugh. "Renew the earth, or so I'm told."

"What?"

I drew out my necklace and unclipped the chain, then placed the effigies on the table between us. I still wasn't sure whether I trusted him enough to tell him everything, or whether I simply wanted to trust *somebody*. Either way, it felt right to bring him into the secret now. "You were asking me about these the other day," I said. Then I launched into the story of how I'd met Granny and Zed on my way to Rockville, and how Granny –

or Kokumthena, the Shawnee Indian creator spirit – had charged me with renewing the earth by setting the people I met on the right path. "But first," I said, "I have to bring my own life into resonance with the spirit, and that involves making some choices." *Three doors will close to you, and you will close three more...* "So far," I finished, "I've shut two of the doors myself."

His expression was unreadable. "Can I ask what they are?"

"I'll tell you one of them," I said. "You know that my boss at the casino refused to give me enough time off to stay with Ruth for as long as she needed me to stay, right?" At his nod, I continued, "I said to Tim that I didn't want to work for a company that valued money over the well-being of its employees. As soon as I said that, I heard what sounded like a door closing very softly."

"And you think…" He let the question hang.

"Right. I closed that door myself. The same thing happened another time when I took action to save myself from a situation that wasn't right for me." I wasn't going to tell him the situation in question involved initiating a relationship with Ruth's surgeon.

"So that's two down and four to go."

"I guess so, yeah."

He seemed on the verge of asking something, but seemed to pivot. "And you closed both of those doors, as opposed to having them closed for you. Is that correct?"

"I believe so. Why?"

He was saved from responding by the arrival of our food. After a few bites of pizza, I resumed my story. "Anyway, as if all that isn't weird enough, I've been having some dreams or visions related to the effigies." I told him about reliving the ceremony inside the Great Circle when I received the turtle in another life, and about seeing my own burial and subsequent exhumation when I found the bird. "Moreover," I said, "these things have been guiding me. You saw the turtle making a racket, right?" He nodded. "It does that when it wants my attention. And if I do what it wants me to do, some of the tarnish melts away."

He swallowed a bite of pizza. "What sorts of things does it want you to do?"

I paused. "Do you think I'm crazy?"

"Well…"

"You do, don't you?" I couldn't help but smile. "Maybe not certifiable, but at least highly imaginative."

"It does seem a little far-fetched," he admitted.

"And yet for some reason," I said, pointing to the effigies, "these two are telling me that you're worthy of my trust."

As if on cue, my turtle lit up with a gentle red-gold glow – low-wattage but unmistakable. As the turtle's light faded, the bird lit up – more golden than red – and scooted as far toward Rick as the chain would allow.

His mouth dropped open. "Um," he said. "You didn't do that, did you?"

"Nope."

"I didn't think you had." He stared at the bird for a moment. "I think I need another beer. You?"

"Yes, please."

He raised a hand to signal the waitress. And as I reached for my necklace, he brushed my hand aside. "Allow me," he said, his voice low. Then he picked it up and he leaned in close to hook it at the back of my neck. Without conscious thought, my fingers gripped his biceps. "You're full of surprises tonight, Maggie May," he said. And stopped.

We faced each other for a long moment – our gazes locked, our lips inches apart. Then he cleared his throat, dropped the refastened chain around my throat, and sat back.

I felt like I'd been kicked. I let go of his arms and tucked my necklace back inside my shirt.

"Sorry," he said, and cleared his throat again.

"It's okay," I said. And because I didn't know what else to do, I picked up the slice of pizza from my plate and resumed eating. In a moment, he did the same.

After a few moments of silent chewing, he said, "I guess I owe you an apology."

I looked up at him. "For what?"

"Kind of leading you on."

I put down my pizza slowly and deliberately. Then I wiped my mouth with the napkin in my lap and put it on the table next to my plate. "In what way?" I asked.

He sighed and threw his napkin on the table, too. "I have to be honest with you, Maggie. I'm not sure I'm ready for a relationship."

"I kind of got that impression from the number of rainchecks you asked for," I said with a small smile. He didn't smile back, though. "Was the divorce that bad?" I asked gently.

"She said some pretty ugly things to me," he admitted. "You know how it is when you're married. You give the other person access to your deepest secrets. You let that person know you, inside and out, in the name of intimacy. Two hearts beating as one, and all that stuff."

"Right."

"And then you split up, and you realize that the only thing you did by baring your soul to that person was to show them all the places they could hurt you." He fiddled with his fork, aligning it this way and that on the tablecloth.

I knew what he meant. "Gene was pretty awful to me, too," I said. "I knew that he was tearing me down to build himself up." His head came up in surprise. "You knew people do that, didn't you? Some just refuse to take responsibility for their failures. Those are the ones who look for someone else to blame."

"Well, yeah, I knew that, but…"

I went on, "Sometimes, of course, failure is just fate. Life just deals you a bad hand at times. But usually, when a relationship goes south, both parties are at fault. And if one of the parties is incapable of introspection – or if both of them are – then you get the drama."

"You said it." He looked away. "I'm just not sure I'll ever be comfortable enough to…"

"To trust again."

"Yeah." He looked at me again. "How do you do that?"

I laughed. "You're asking the wrong person, my friend."

He didn't laugh, but he nodded. "Friends. I like that. We could just be friends for a while."

"Sure," I said, sighing inwardly. I was definitely developing deeper feelings for Rick. But from what I was hearing, he might never again be willing to commit to the level of trust that a relationship required, and so I wondered whether I should just end this now.

If either my turtle or my bird had an opinion on the question, though, neither was willing to share it just then.

"Guess we should get the rest of this to go, huh?" I said.

He downed the last of his beer in a gulp. "Sorry. I guess I wasn't much in the mood for pizza, after all."

We regained a bit of levity on the ride home – making jokes about the other drivers and the billboards we passed – and it was only a little bit forced. Still, I was grateful when Rick made the turn onto Mom's block.

He slowed down as we approached the driveway, and was about to turn in when I caught movement out of the corner of my eye: a car pulling away from the curb on the other side of the street. The SUV passed Rick's car as it took off down the block. "Is that Sandy?" Rick asked.

I studied the back of the vehicle as it moved away. "It is," I confirmed. "What's he doing here, anyway?"

Rick parked and turned off the engine. "Let's find out."

Mom was watching TV when we came in. She muted the sound and gave us a sunny smile. "There you are! Did you two have a nice time?"

"Yeah, we did," I half-lied. I traded a look with Rick as he scooted past me to put the leftover pizza in the fridge. "Mom, was Sandy here?"

She looked puzzled. "When?"

"Earlier tonight. Maybe just a few minutes ago."

She considered the question. "I don't believe so. Why?"

"We thought we saw his car leaving just now," Rick said.

"From here?"

"Parked across the street," I said.

"That's odd. What would he be doing here?" she asked.

"That's what we're trying to figure out." I slipped out of my coat and hung it on the hall tree by the door. "You're sure he didn't come in."

"Sure, I'm sure," she said. "I've been sitting right here the whole time. I would have seen him if he'd come in."

Rick approached me. "I'm going to take a little walk around outside, if that's okay."

"Want me to come with you?"

"No, you stay here. Be right back." He slid past me and went out.

Mom and I traded a glance. "He's a good man," she said.

"Rick? Yeah, he is." I perched on the arm of the couch.

A few minutes later, he came back in. He stamped snow from his shoes as he said, "I didn't see anything unusual, but of course it's hard to tell with just a phone flashlight."

"I'll take a better look in the morning, when it's light," I said. "Thanks for checking."

"You bet. Well." He hunched his shoulders and gave me a sidelong glance. "Thanks for dinner. It was...memorable."

My mouth quirked up on one side. Then I said, "You sure you don't want the rest of the pizza?"

"No," he said, raising one hand. "You and your mom enjoy it." He hesitated, then leaned over and kissed my cheek. "Goodnight, Maggie. Goodnight, Mrs. Muir." Then he fled.

As I shut the door after him, Mom laughed. "What did you do to the poor man?"

I shrugged and shook my head. "I don't think he's ever gotten over his wife leaving him the way she did. And then his parents dying on top of it." I sat on the couch. "That's a lot to process."

"He's had some time to do it," Mom said. "You think he'll ever be done?"

"I don't know, Mom." I didn't tell her that I'd been asking myself the same question.

"Well, I'm sure you can help him get over it, if anybody can," she said.

I laughed. "I'm sorry, but I think you have me confused with Bea."

"No, I mean it. Look how you handled that awful ex-mother-in-law of yours. When you moved back here right after you divorced Gene, all your father and I ever heard about was how Ruth did this and Ruth did that to you and the kids. But this time, you practically had her eating out of your hand."

"I wouldn't go that far," I protested.

"Think about it," Mom said. "Bea had to have gotten her counseling talent from somewhere, and it sure as heck wasn't from her father's side of the family."

"Mom!" I said, but I was laughing.

"Well, it's true," she said. "I never liked any of the Brandts. Except for Abby – Abby is okay."

"Good to know," I said, getting up. "I'm going to head for bed."

"Goodnight," she said, as I bent over to hug her.

I'm not sure why, but I snapped on the hallway light as I headed to my room. I didn't, usually – having grown up in the house, I had muscle memory of how many steps it took to get to my bedroom door, and even where the subfloor squeaked. But something prompted me to flip on that light – and the same something, whatever it was, prompted me to glance toward my brother's old room before turning into mine.

I paused. My boxes had been moved.

I was sure I'd stacked them just inside the door. But now they were pushed out, and the stacks were askew.

I went back out into the living room. "Did you move any of my boxes, Mom?"

She had gone back to watching her show. "No," she said, distracted. "Maybe Sandy did. He was in there looking for something."

"But you said he wasn't here today," I said, my gut churning.

She paused and looked at me as if I'd caught her in a lie. "Maybe it was a different day."

"Mom," I said, keeping a lid on my anger, "was Sandy here today or not?"

"What difference does it make?" she said irritably. "He's welcome to come and go in this house, the same as you are."

As far as I was concerned, he was *not* welcome to come and go in this house – but memory-challenged or no, Mom was still making the rules.

And about those memory issues: she'd been better over the past couple of days. I remembered Ruth's memory was worse when her stress level had maxed out, and wondered what – or who – was stressing Mom out and making her forget things again.

She was old. A lot was going on. I decided not to make her life worse with accusations I couldn't prove – yet.

"Goodnight, Mom," I said, and went back to Sandy's room. I restacked the boxes along the wall, checking each one to see whether there was any evidence of tampering – although what my brother would want with extra blankets and a seven-piece cookware set, I couldn't begin to guess.

None of the boxes appeared to have been opened. When I found the box of baby things and realized the packing tape was intact, I let out a breath that I hadn't known I was holding.

I restacked everything neatly except for that box, which I brought into my room and stored in the back of my closet. It didn't escape my notice that I'd just done exactly what Ruth and Arnie had done with their box full of Lenny's keepsakes. The difference, I reasoned, was that my box held no secrets.

Chapter 13

With some misgivings, I went back to work the following day. I really wanted to stay home in case Sandy showed up again – which he could do at any time. After all, as a retiree, however "disabled," he had all hours of the day and night free. But I had zero vacation time accrued – and if I did stay home, what would I do the next day? And the day after that? I couldn't risk getting fired again for not showing up to work – not while my former supervisor at the casino was still spreading horrible stories around about me. And he was; I had it on good authority from my boss, Ron. I needed to build a track record for showing up that would disprove the lies Dee was spreading.

And if I lost this job, Sandy would be all over me for screwing up my life again. Not that I was trying to please him or gain his favor. I just didn't want to hear it.

So I prominently displayed my cell phone number on the fridge, and told Mom to call me if anything concerned her. "I can be home in fifteen minutes if you need me," I said as I got ready to walk out the door.

"You don't have to worry about me," she said. "I can take care of myself."

"I know you can. This is just in case. See you tonight." And with my stomach roiling, I forced myself to walk out the door and get in my car.

Work engaged my brain sufficiently that when lunchtime rolled around, I realized I hadn't worried about Mom all morning. And Sandy didn't show up that day, or the next day, or the next. After that, I started to relax. And I breathed a little easier when I got home each day and found that everything was fine.

It was one night that week when Riley called me, out of the blue. "I talked to Abby," she said. "They had a real nice time with you and your mom."

"It was great seeing them. And the baby is adorable."

"I know! I've seen the pictures. They're coming here for New Year's. I can't wait!"

I pictured her sitting at the dinette set she had bought, in the kitchen of the house in which I had raised my kids. She was such a tiny thing, short and slender, with long, dark hair. She would have her legs crossed twice, knee and ankle, and would be gesturing madly with the hand that wasn't holding the phone to her ear. "How are you doing, Riley?" I asked.

"To be honest? I've been better. But I didn't call to talk about me. I wanted to find out how *you* were doing."

"Oh, fine," I said. "I'm a shift manager at the local grocery store, and..."

"That's not what I mean," she said. "How's that stuff with your brother going?"

Of course she'd know. She'd talked to Abby. "Okay so far," I said. "We haven't heard from him since we put the house in a trust."

"That was really smart," she said. "Did you think of that, or did the lawyer?"

"He did," I said. "Rick. Rick did." When I said his name aloud, it was like it ruptured a dam. For the next few minutes, I poured out my heart to Riley: my nascent feelings for Rick, our history, his fears of commitment, and my misgivings about pursuing the relationship.

"Wow," she said when I'd wound down.

I swiped at my eyes with the back of my hand and grimaced. "Sorry. I shouldn't have bent your ear about this."

"No, it's fine."

"I just don't have anybody here to *talk* to." I couldn't exactly talk about my love life – or lack of one – with my co-workers, as I was their supervisor. And there was only so much I felt comfortable telling Mom about. It just seemed odd to me that a fifty-eight-year-old woman would be asking her mother for dating advice.

"I know. Abby said you seemed kind of lonely."

I opened my mouth to protest, and then closed it. Was I? Was that why I had glommed onto Rick? Was that why I was pushing him into something he said he wasn't ready for? "Maybe," I allowed. "It's just me and Mom here. I used to go out sometimes with a couple of my co-workers at the casino, but I haven't heard from them since I got back from Maryland."

"You should call them," she said. "Invite them out for a drink or something."

"I should," I agreed, although my heart wasn't in it. I couldn't help thinking Dee had turned them against me, too.

"So anyway, your brother," she said. "What's his name? Sandy?"

"What about him?"

"I was thinking about it after I talked to Abby. She said he was pretty rough on you when you were kids."

"He's a jerk," I said. It came out more forcefully than I'd intended. Maybe opening up about Rick really had burst a dam; a lot of stuff was bubbling to the surface now. "He did everything he could think of to make my life miserable. And he would say horrible stuff to me. He had me convinced I was a failure, no matter what I did." I laughed bitterly. "It's funny, but I didn't realize how much of a shadow he had cast over my life until he moved out. I probably never would have applied to college, even, if he'd still been living at home."

"Yeah," she said. "And I wonder…"

I was suddenly eager to hear what she had to say. "What?"

"Well, it just occurred to me. When you first moved here with Gene, you pretty much let Ruth run roughshod over you."

"Yeah, but I was young," I said. "I was just barely out of my teens."

She plunged ahead in a rush. "Right, I know, but I wonder whether you weren't sort of primed to take what Ruth was dishing out because Sandy had set you up for it."

I had been lounging on my bed while we talked, but that made me sit up straight. "Holy cow. I never thought about it before, but you're right."

Then I gasped as a red-gold pattern began to glow in the air before me, as if someone had turned up a dimmer switch. I could see my childhood clearly, and where Sandy's influence had pushed me off the path I was meant to take. With his departure, I regained the path – only to be knocked sideways again by Ruth, and then by Gene's philandering. I could see the spot where I left Rockville, too – but I was troubled by it, because I could see that I had never fully regained my true path. The work I'd done in Rockville recently had nudged me closer to the mark. But now I was veering away from it again – and guess who was applying the pressure?

"I need to cut ties with him," I said, and blinked. The map hadn't changed, but it looked different to me now – as well as more familiar. I pulled out my turtle and held it up to the glowing path before me. Sure enough, the midair map was a match for the pattern on the turtle's back.

"Maggie?" Riley said. "Are you still there?"

"Yeah." I swallowed. "Sorry. What you said really hit home." The map before my eyes faded out as the turtle began to heat up in my hand. I watched as the verdigris on her back retreated to the point where I could easily make out the map. I blinked again and tucked the necklace back inside my shirt. Its warmth comforted me. "Sandy has been a thorn in my side my whole life. I need to…" I stopped. "But I can't."

"What? You can't what?"

I did my best to articulate the associations tumbling into place. "See, I escaped from Ruth by running away. But I can't run away this time. I have to stay here and help Mom."

"Running away didn't solve anything last time, anyway," she pointed out. "You had to come back eventually to sort it out."

"I did, didn't I? Huh. How did you get so smart about this stuff, anyway?"

I could hear the smile in her voice. "It's from hanging around with Bea. It rubs off."

"I guess it does. Nice job."

"Thanks. And also it helps to not be directly involved. It's a lot easier to see patterns in other people's lives."

"Also very true." I grinned. "Maybe you should think about taking up counseling yourself."

"Maybe." She sighed.

"That was a pretty big sigh," I said. "Come on, tell me. What's going on? You said you'd been better."

"Yeah." She sighed again. "Yeah. I could use a little help with the big picture myself."

"Shoot." I settled back on the bed.

It took a little more coaxing, but I finally got the story out of her. Basically, Gene had moved most of his stuff home to Ruth's, and Riley was now rambling around the four-bedroom split-level where I'd raised my kids all by herself. "It doesn't even feel like my house now," she said.

"Whose does it feel like?"

"*I* don't know," she said. "Bea's and Emily's and Tim's, I guess. Or yours."

"Okay, wait. It's definitely not mine," I said with a laugh.

That made her laugh, too. "I know that up here." I imagined her tapping her skull with one finger. "But my heart isn't sure it belongs here any more."

My own heart went out to her. "How do we end up like this?" I said. "In places where we don't belong?"

"I wish I knew."

We sat quietly for a moment. Then I said, "Where does your heart say you belong?"

"I don't know," she said, but it sounded like she was hedging. I was about to call her on it, but she abruptly changed the subject. "Anyway, Gene has agreed to go into an in-patient treatment thing. He's turning over the running of the store to his assistant manager while he takes a sabbatical."

"A *sabbatical?*" I said skeptically.

"That's what he's calling it. The treatment program is in Cincinnati. I thought you'd want to know."

"Thanks for the heads-up," I said. Cincinnati was close, but it was also a big place. I figured it would be easy enough to avoid him. "So. You think this program will work?"

"Honestly, Maggie? I don't know. It's not like he's jumping at the chance to reform. Bea and John found the program for him, and they told him if he didn't agree to go, they were going to turn him in."

"Good for them," I said. Because of the nature of their work, Bea and John both had an ethical duty to report pedophiles to the authorities. "I hope he knows the kind of chance they're taking for him."

"I'm not sure it matters to hm."

I thought about his behavior over the years, and shook my head. "You're probably right. Unfortunately. When does he go?"

"Next Monday. He tried to talk them into letting him stay home for another few weeks, but Bea put her foot down."

"Good for her." My eldest daughter had more intestinal fortitude than I did. I might have let him have that extra couple of weeks. But of course, then he'd have another excuse for putting it off. "So where does all this leave you?"

"I'm not sure. Maggie?" She paused. "I don't know that I want to stay married to him."

"Having been in your shoes, I can tell you that I completely understand."

She laughed a little. "I thought maybe you would."

"Could you move home with your parents?" It occurred to me as I said it that I didn't know anything about Riley's family. The subject had never come up.

"Nah. I mean, I could, but I wouldn't. I'd probably get an apartment or something. That's not what's bugging me."

"So what's bugging you?"

"It's that part about 'in sickness and in health.'"

"Ah."

"How did you get past that?"

The answer came easily to me. "When I left, I believed I was running for my life. Cleaving to him seemed pointless when he was part of the problem. And besides, he'd broken our marriage vows long before I left." I paused. "I don't know that any of that applies to your situation, though."

"Yeah, see, that's just it. I knew what he was when I married him."

"But you didn't know the whole story," I said. "You didn't know about Debbie."

"That's true." She sighed. "I don't know. I guess I have a couple of months to figure it out, though."

"Talk to Bea," I suggested. "I don't think she can take you on as a patient, but she could refer you to somebody."

"I will. And you should be talking to somebody, too," she said.

I shrugged. "Probably."

"At least promise me you'll call some of those ladies you used to go out with," she said. "Don't isolate yourself. And don't depend on Rick to be your whole social circle."

"Yes, ma'am," I said good-naturedly.

"Oh, all right," she said, relenting. "I'll let you go. Thanks for listening."

"Thank *you* for calling," I said. "It was just what I needed."

We said goodbye and I ended the call. Then I took off my necklace and placed it on the nightstand. I traced with my forefinger the map on my turtle's back, marveling that a design created so many centuries ago could reflect what was happening in my life here and now. Although it didn't, exactly, because I'd deviated from the path. But now I could see how much I needed to get back to it.

And how to do it. I knew in my gut that I was going to have to cut Sandy out of my life. I just wasn't sure how to accomplish it when I was living with Mom. It would be a mercy if I could keep him away from her, too – but I was certain she wouldn't agree, and I didn't know how to convince her I was right.

Chapter 14

I decided to broach the subject when I got home from work the next night. Mom typically wasn't awake yet when I left for work — quite the turnaround from when I was younger and she was always the first one out of bed, making breakfast for Dad and getting us all out the door for the day. I wondered whether she was slowing down naturally, or whether the drugs she had been on were still affecting her sleep — or whether she was just sick of always being the first one up.

In any case, I got home from work that night and started dinner, as it was my turn to cook. I had already started frying the pork chops and boiling the potatoes when she came into the kitchen.

"Smells good," she said, peering into the pans. "Mmm, pork chops. Don't undercook them this time. I was afraid to eat them last time."

"Why?"

"You know why, Maggie. You have to cook pork until it's well done because of trichinosis."

"Not any more."

She looked at me as if I'd lost my mind. "You're kidding."

"Nope. The experts say it's okay for pork chops and roasts to be a little pink."

"When did that start?"

"Years ago. When pork producers stopped feeding worm-infested meat scraps to their pigs."

Mom made a face. "That sounds horrible."

I turned off the heat under the potatoes and drained the water from the pan. "It was. That's why they quit doing it. Would you get me the butter and milk, please?"

She brought me the items from the fridge. "You could have told me before, you know."

I did – the last time I made pork chops. And the time before that. But I didn't see any point in scolding her. Instead, I said, "Well, I'm telling you now," and attacked the potatoes with the masher.

"You could use the mixer for that," Mom said.

I stopped and gave her my best *you're getting on my last nerve* look. "Do you want to do this?"

"Certainly not," she said primly. "It's your turn to cook." She got two plates from the cabinet and began setting the table. "I'm just saying."

I ignored her. Mashing potatoes by hand helped me work out some of my irritation on nights like this – which was nearly every night that it was my turn to cook.

At last we sat down to eat. She eyed the pink in the center of her pork chop, glanced askance at me, and ate it anyway. I mentally declared victory – even though I knew I'd have to fight the same battle again next time.

As we were finishing our meal, I braced myself for the storm I was about to cause. "Have you heard from Sandy?" I asked, striving to sound like I was just making conversation.

She gave me the side-eye. "Why?"

"Just wondering. I'm still concerned that he was here the other day and told you not to tell me."

"He didn't tell me not to tell you. I just forgot, that's all." She chased her last kernel of corn around on her plate.

"Did he try to get you to give him the house again?"

She tried scooping up the errant kernel with her fork, but it didn't work. She paused and looked at me. "What's this all about?"

"I don't trust him," I said. *Might as well just lay it out there.* "He's an addict and so is Diane. You know that, Mom – they've overdosed right in front of you. And you know they need money to buy drugs, and that disability check of Sandy's isn't going to stretch far enough to cover it."

She attacked the kernel with her fork again, this time by attempting to spear it – but all that did was squeeze out the innards. She sighed and put down the fork. "What are you driving at?"

I took a breath. "I don't want him here any more."

"Here we go," she muttered.

"Mom, he's been abusive to me my whole life. And he's abused you, too." I was getting louder, as if that would help to make her understand me. "He's already tried to take the house away from you. What's next? Your savings? Your Social Security check?"

"Don't raise your voice to me," she said. "You've never liked him. You always play the victim when it comes to him."

My eyes widened. "Mom, it's not 'playing the victim' if you're actually being victimized."

She scooped up the mangled piece of corn with her spoon, and pointed it at me. "You need to promise me something," she said.

I was wary of her change of topic. "What is it?"

"You need to promise that you will get along with your brother. No matter what it takes."

"Why on earth would I do that?" I asked, incredulous.

"Because when I'm gone, he's all you'll have left," she said, and popped the spoon into her mouth.

I understood what she was saying: We had no other living relatives on either her side or Dad's. If Mom passed away, Sandy would be my only connection to my family of origin.

But I had other family – my kids. And they treated me a lot better than my brother ever had.

"No," I said. "I will not promise you that. I won't be locked into a relationship with an abuser in the name of keeping this family together."

I heard a door shut firmly. I didn't go looking for it – it wasn't in this house.

"Well," Mom said after a moment of silence. "I hope you don't regret it."

"I don't believe I will."

Two nights later, we got a call on the landline from Diane's older sister Jane, telling us Diane was dead. "It was that horrible fentanyl," she said. "She shot up while Sandy was out getting groceries, but the shot was laced with fentanyl and she didn't know it. By the time he got home, it was too late, even for the antidote." Her voice broke. "I wish to God her plastic surgeon had never put her on that stuff."

"That's terrible," I said. "I'm so sorry to hear it."

Mom was on the extension in her bedroom. "Why didn't Sandy call us himself?"

"He's really torn up about it," she said. "He's not coping very well right now, so he asked me to let you know."

"My poor, dear boy," Mom said, and began to cry.

"When's the funeral?" I asked. I didn't really want to go, but I knew Mom would, and that meant I would have to drive her.

"Thursday morning at ten," Jane said, and gave me the name of the funeral home.

So the morning of New Year's Eve, we drove up to the west side of Indianapolis to pay our final respects to my sister-in-law. "Tell me again why we're going," I said, looking for the exit off I-70.

"Where?" Mom asked.

"To Diane's funeral."

"Oh. Did she die?"

"Yeah. Drug overdose."

"Oh."

Ten minutes later, as I navigated city streets to get to the funeral home, Mom said, "How long before we're home?"

"Depends on how long the funeral takes," I said.

"What funeral?"

"Diane's."

"Did she die?"

I didn't bother responding. I was tired of repeating myself, and cranky from having to miss work to be here at all. Besides, we'd arrived at our destination. Mom would figure it out soon enough.

Sandy, dressed in a black shirt and dress pants with brown loafers, saw us come in. He broke away from a couple I didn't know to come over to us. "What the hell are you doing here?" he growled.

"Mom's here for *you*," I said, adding *you ungrateful wretch* in my head.

He was working himself up into a righteous rage. "I can't believe the two of you would show your faces here at all," he said. "It's your fault she's dead."

Mom stepped back, shocked. "How can you say that?"

"You're saying we shoved the junk down her throat?" I asked. "Or what?"

"For your information, I was going to put my wife into a treatment program with the money from the house," he hissed. "Then you and Baby Huey had to screw it all up. And now she's *dead*." He gritted his teeth.

I said pleasantly, "That's an impressive display of blame-shifting."

"If you needed money," Mom said, "why didn't you just ask me? I would have given it to you if you'd asked."

"Because I would have demanded proof," I said, keeping my eyes on Sandy. "Which program? How much would it cost? And how come only Diane was going? What about you, brother dear? You have a problem, too."

"Goddamn you," he said, and drew back a fist.

In a flash, my hand came up. But I didn't just block the blow. Somehow, I managed to push back – hard enough that he stumbled backwards and nearly fell. A few people nearby gasped.

With murder in his eye, he squared his shoulders and raised his fist again.

"Hey, now," someone said, and two large men in suits and ties – employees of the funeral home, I assumed – grabbed my brother by either arm. "This is a trying time for everyone," one of them said, "but there's no reason to get physical." He looked at us. "Can I ask your relationship to Mrs. Muir?"

Mom spoke up. "She's my daughter-in-law. He's my son." She nodded at Sandy, who struggled with his captors. "And this is my daughter Maggie, his sister."

"We're just here to pay our respects," I put in. "We can sit in the back."

"Is that okay with you, Mr. Muir?"

Sandy had stopped struggling, but he was still glaring at me. "Fine," he said, and shook loose of the two men. "Don't either of you come near me." He turned on his heel and stalked away.

"Hey, you came up to us," I said. He stopped in mid-stalk. I assumed he was mulling over whether to turn back and take another jab at me. But then he kept going.

"Grief does funny things to people," the man said.

"Sorry to have caused a scene," I said. Mom was looking anxiously at Sandy's retreating back.

"To be honest, this is nothing," he said. "We've had some doozies here over the years. Now, why don't you two ladies sit right here." Smiling, he indicated chairs very close to the door. "You'll be able to hear and see everything just fine, and you can scoot out first, as the service is wrapping up."

"Sounds good," I said. "Thank you."

"My pleasure," he said, and walked away.

"Who knew funeral homes had bouncers?" I said. "Let's take our seats, Mom."

"Can't we go up and pay our respects to Diane?" she asked.

Sandy had taken a seat in the first row, his rigid back to us. I told Mom, "I think that would be a very bad idea under the circumstances. Anyway, I don't think there's anything to see. Looks like it's a closed casket."

Organ music began playing. Mom nodded to me. Presently, she said, "The flowers are very pretty."

"Yes, they are."

A moment later, Diane's sister Jane took a seat next to me. "I feel like I should apologize for Sandy," she said in an undertone. "He's just so upset."

"You don't have to make excuses for him," I said, more tartly than I meant to.

"Thank you, dear," Mom said, and patted Jane on the arm.

"Sorry," I said. "It's a trying time for all of us. And I'm very sorry for your loss."

"She was such a wonderful person," said Jane. "We were very close, growing up – well, you know. It's just been in these last few years that…" Her eyes reddened and she reached in her purse for a tissue.

"It's a horrible thing," I said. "I wish Sandy would give them up."

"I'll pay for treatment for him," Mom said. "All he has to do is ask."

Jane smiled at her. "Thank you, Shirley. I'll tell him." She glanced at the front of the room, where it appeared the service was about to start. "Thanks for coming." She gave us each a hug and scooted back to her seat near the front.

As the pastor talked about how Diane had been a loving wife and daughter, I found myself musing about Sandy's attempt to hit me, and how easy it was for me to rebuff him. I'd had a similar experience in Rockville a few months before, when Gene tried to make a pass at me and went sprawling when I strong-armed him. At the time, I'd assumed that I'd just pushed him harder than I'd meant to. But I hadn't pushed at all this time – I'd only meant to block Sandy's punch – and still he nearly went down. *Did you do that?* I asked my turtle.

In response, I saw in my mind's eye a red-gold glow surrounding me – my own personal turtle-shell-shaped force field. I gathered it would repel anyone who meant me harm. "Cool," I murmured.

"Be quiet," Mom hissed.

"Yes, ma'am," I said. It was good to know I had some protection against bullies, but I didn't intend to test it by going out and looking for trouble.

At the end of the service, when the organ music began playing again (I didn't see a live organist, so I suspected it was recorded), the nice bouncer approached us and escorted us out. He was pleasant about it, and made us feel like he was there for our protection — but I was certain the ulterior motive was to keep us separated from Sandy, in case he decided to throw another punch at me.

Back in the car, I suggested to Mom that we stop for lunch before we got on the road for home. Inside the restaurant, while we perused the menu, I said, "That was a lovely service, wasn't it?"

"Sure." She flipped the menu over. "Who was it for?"

"Mom, it was for Diane."

She looked up at me in surprise. "Oh, no. Did she die?"

Chapter 15

I was done with Sandy, but he wasn't done with me.

The day after New Year's, I had to work a double shift. Our evening manager had the night off for some family event, and there was no one else to take his shift – so I agreed to stay on. As a middle manager, I wouldn't get paid overtime for staying, but I didn't feel like I had a choice. I realized when I agreed to stay that I was doing the same thing I'd done when Ruth demanded that I stay with her in Rockville while she underwent cancer treatment, but I consoled myself with the fact that this was going to be an extra six hours, not two months – and I was unlikely to lose a job over it.

I was exhausted by the end of that long day, and my feet hurt from standing. I wanted nothing more than a hot bath and my bed. But as I drove up to the house, I saw Sandy's SUV parked in my spot in the driveway. My stomach clenched. I parked at the curb, slammed the door, and hurried up the sidewalk, afraid of what I might find inside.

Usually Mom left a lamp on in the living room for me, but tonight the house was dark. I flipped the wall switch by the front door, but nothing happened. "Mom?" I called out.

"Keep your voice down," my brother said from the direction of the bedrooms. "Mom's asleep."

"Is the power out?"

"No." With my eyes adjusted to the dark, I could see him – a looming shadow just inside the hallway.

"Why aren't the lights working, then?"

"I flipped the breaker." There was an ugly edge to his voice.

"Why?"

He swaggered toward me. "You and I need to have this out, Maggie. I don't want you here. You're screwing up my relationship with Mom, trying to turn her against me."

"You can't say I don't have good reason," I said, edging back toward the door.

"You've always been her favorite," he said, adopting a mewling tone. "Maggie this and Maggie that. Oh, Maggie is so smart! Oh, Maggie is so pretty!"

"What are you talking about? Mom never said any of that stuff to me."

"She said it to *me*," he said. "She thought the sun and moon revolved around you. I couldn't *wait* to get out of here."

"And then you did. End of story." I backed up against the front door, which I'd shut before I realized the lights were out.

"But you keep coming back," he said. "And she keeps letting you back in. You're a grown woman and she's still supporting you."

"I have a job," I said. "I'm supporting myself, thank you very much. And none of that is any business of yours, anyway."

"It is when you're making her spend my half of the inheritance on *you*." He took another step toward me.

"This is about *money?*" I said. "Is that why you thought you were entitled to the house? Because you thought I was spending all of Mom's cash?"

"I know you are," he said. "Don't try to deny it. And I need the money worse than you do. I'm sick! You're just lazy!"

"You're not sick – you're a junkie," I spat. "There's a difference." In a less heated moment, I would have said drug addiction *is* an illness. But I wasn't inclined to reason with him just then, and he was past the point of reason anyway.

"You're in my way, brat," he said, and took another step toward me. "And it ends tonight. I've been waiting for hours for you. Where have you been – screwing Baby Huey?"

"None of your business," I said, sneaking my hand behind my back. If I could get hold of the door handle, I could get out of the house, get back in my car, and get out of here. Then I could call the cops. A judge would have to give me a restraining order after this – and there was nothing Mom could say that would stop me from pursuing one.

"Doesn't matter. It gave me plenty of time to shut off the power and unplug the phone," he said. "And I made sure Mom took a couple of extra sleeping pills, too. She'll never hear you." He stepped toward me again. "I hope it was really good sex, little sister, because it's the last time you'll ever get laid."

I grabbed the door handle and twisted. He lunged for the opening door and slammed it shut again. "Oh, no, you don't," he breathed in my ear. "You're not getting away from me this time. With you out of the picture, I'll inherit everything. All I have to do is lock Mom up and drug her up good. Maybe I'll get her hooked on fentanyl. What do you think, Maggie? Would that be a fitting end for her?"

"You'd do that to your own mother," I said, aghast. "You worthless scumbag."

He closed both hands around my throat.

That is, he tried to. A flash of red-gold sent him crashing into the easy chair near the door, upsetting the lamp on the side table and knocking it to the floor. I heard the bulb shatter. "You broke Mom's lamp," I said. "She's gonna be so mad at you!"

He staggered to his feet. "I'm going to kill you if it's the last thing I do!" he roared, and came at me again.

From out of nowhere came the sound of wings. Flames of red and gold seemed to dance along the walls, and something – some presence – said, in a voice I'd heard in a dream, "I told you, Mishepeshu. It wasn't a threat."

Then Sandy lit up in flames for real. He screamed and ran down the hallway toward the bathroom.

"Sandy!" I cried, and started to go after him.

"Nokomtha! You must leave!" the dream-voice shouted. Smoke was filling the room; even the carpet was beginning to smoke. The door behind me banged open, seemingly of its own accord – and with the sudden influx of oxygen, the whole place went up in flames.

Something pushed me out through the open doorway. I found myself sprawled, face-down, on the frozen grass. I struggled to push myself to my knees, gasping at the pain from my back. "Mom!" I cried. "Sandy!" But there was no reaching either of them now.

Heat washed over me, and I knew I needed to move farther from the house. I cried out as I got to my feet and, coughing, stumbled to the curb. Just as I thought of calling 911, I realized a neighbor must have beaten me to it, because no sooner had my fingers touched the phone in my pocket than I heard sirens.

Even so, by the time they got there, the place was a total loss. With the slam of a virtual door reverberating in my head, I leaned against my car and watched my childhood home burn to the ground.

The Red Cross was wonderful. Before the hospital discharged me – I spent a week there for treatment of the burns on my back – they had found me a motel room, the beginnings of a new wardrobe, and a referral for counseling.

Ron Olsen was also wonderful. He ordered a new set of uniforms without docking my pay for them. I was grateful to him for that, but more so for the three weeks off with pay. He called it bereavement leave, but I'd read the employee handbook, so I knew the company's policy was paltry couple of days.

The police were not so wonderful. An officer visited me in the hospital to interview me about what had happened. I could hardly tell them the real course of events – that a Native American thunderbird spirit believed my brother to be an underwater panther and fried him when he attacked me – so I hedged a little. I mean, I still told the truth about what happened that night; I just left out the supernatural stuff. But the cop must have noticed my hesitation, because he was back the next day with another cop. At that point, I told them I wasn't going to say anything else without my lawyer present.

That meant I had to call Rick. But I knew I was going to have to talk to him sooner or later anyway – he was Mom's estate attorney, after all. I was just nervous about it, after the way we'd left things the last time I saw him.

To his credit, he was totally professional. "I'll call them and set up a time for the interview," he said. "Are you up to it?"

I'd progressed by then from lying flat on my belly to sitting up in a chair, which didn't hurt too badly if I was careful not to squirm. "Depends on how long it takes," I said.

"Tell you what. You raise your hand when you're ready to take a break, and I'll make sure they understand what it means."

"Sounds good." I paused. "Criminal law isn't really your thing, is it?"

"Actually," he said, "it was my specialty, back in the day. What makes you ask?"

"What makes me ask?" I said. "They think I set the fire, don't they?"

"Maybe. Maybe not. Our job right now is to convince them you didn't."

So the following day, my traveling IV stand and I entertained the two cops and Rick in the patient lounge at the end of my hall. An orderly set up a screen so we had a little privacy.

Officer Pauley, who had come to see me first, was fairly young and tall; he stood next to the screen, presumably to wave off anyone who wanted to see what was happening behind it. Detective Andriotti was shorter and had dark hair that was going gray; I thought he might be in his forties. He took a seat next to Rick and asked all the questions.

"Ms. Muir," he began, "tell me what happened on the night of the fire."

"I've already told your partner there," I said, nodding toward a stone-faced Officer Pauley.

"Tell us again, then."

I glanced at Rick, who didn't object. So I breathed in and began. "I got home late…"

"Why?"

"I had pulled a double shift at work that day."

"Where do you work?"

"At the grocery store."

"And what do you do there?"

"I'm a shift manager. Mr. Olsen is the store manager and my boss." I glared at him. "Do you want to hear what happened, or are you going to keep interrupting me?"

He spread his arms wide, palms up. "Apologies, ma'am. Please proceed."

I cut a glance at Rick and caught him smirking, which told me I was on the right track. "Thank you," I said, with a touch of asperity. "As I was saying, I got home very late from work – after nine o'clock. Sandy's SUV was parked in my space in the driveway, so I knew he was there."

"Sandy is…?"

"Sandy *was* my brother," I said.

"My condolences," said the detective in a perfunctory manner. "How would you characterize your relationship with your brother?"

"He was a jerk," I said bluntly.

"How so?"

"He was verbally abusive to me from childhood on," I said. "More recently, he and his wife became hooked on opioids, and he had concocted a plot to get Mom to sign the house over to him so he could take out a mortgage on it to pay for drugs."

"But that didn't happen."

"Nope," I said. "Rick helped Mom put the house in a trust."

Andriotti turned to Rick. "How was this trust supposed to work? What would trigger it?"

"The trust provided that Mrs. Muir had the use and enjoyment of the property until her death, at which time the property would pass into her estate," said Rick. "I'd be happy to provide you with a copy of the document."

"That would be great, thanks. And her heirs were these two? Anybody else?"

"No," said Rick. "Just Sandy and Maggie."

"And Mr. Muir knew all that."

"He was provided with a courtesy copy of both the trust document and his mother's will, yes."

I wanted to hug Rick. It couldn't have been clearer that Sandy was the one with the motive to kill both Mom and me.

But Andriotti wasn't done. "Ms. Muir," he said, "how did the fire start?"

This was where I'd had to get creative. "I told your officer," I said. "My brother had me trapped against the front door. He tried to choke me, but I fought free. He knocked over a lamp and the bulb broke. It must have been a spark from that that set the place on fire. Then when I opened the front door to leave, the whole house went up."

"Backdraft," he said.

"I believe that's what it's called, yes."

He looked hard at me. "You're sure that's what happened."

I matched his gaze. "Look, detective, a lot was going on. All I know is that one minute, I was fighting to draw breath, and managed to knock my brother off of me – and the next minute the house was burning down around me. So I got out."

He continued the staring contest. "So you're saying you don't know how the fire started?"

"That's right."

"Because a neighbor told us he heard screams coming from the house, and a bright light moving from the living room to the bedrooms, before you came out through the front door."

I drew upright, wincing at the pain from my sudden movement. "Detective Andriotti, are you suggesting that I set my brother on fire?"

He shrugged. "It fits, doesn't it? He was threatening you and your mother. You could have wanted him gone."

"But Mom was asleep in the house!" I said.

Rick cut in. "Don't say anything else, Maggie."

"No, Rick," I said. "I want this straightened out right now." I turned to the detective. "You're not thinking this through. If I had wanted to kill my brother, there are a hundred other ways. The easiest way would have been to leave him alone and let him OD again. It wouldn't have been his first. And his wife died from one just a couple of weeks ago."

The two cops exchanged a glance. "Where was this?" Andriotti asked.

"Indianapolis," I said. "Feel free to check it out. But that's beside the point. Detective Andriotti, I lived with my mother. And I loved her." My voice caught. I cleared my throat and went on, "I would not have burned down my own home and killed my own mother just to get my brother out of my life."

The detective looked again at his buddy, and rose. "Thank you, Ms. Muir. We'll be in touch." He joined the officer at the screen, and then turned back. "One other thing. Were you wearing a red garment that night?"

"A red…?" I was bewildered. "No. Why?"

"Because the neighbor who heard the screams saw you come out of the house. He told me it looked like you had something red on your back."

"Must have been a trick of the light," Rick said. "Thank you, officers."

"We'll be in touch," said Andriotti, and they left.

Rick waited to make sure they were gone. Then he took my hand. "You're shaking. Are you okay?"

I hadn't realized I was trembling until he mentioned it. "Yeah, I guess. I should have done what you told me, huh?"

He blew out a breath. "Yeah. But it was fine. You didn't say anything to hurt your case." He eyed me. "What do you suppose the red on your back was?"

"Help me back to my room, would you?" I said. He helped me up from the chair and let me lean on him as I wheeled the IV stand back to my room. We were nearly there when we found my necklace lying in the hallway.

"Oh, for God's sake," I muttered, bending to scoop it up and hissing with the sudden movement.

"You took it off?" Rick said, his eyes on the necklace as he helped me ease myself upright again.

"Come on in. Shut the door." As he did so, I eased myself into bed and leaned back against the pillows with my eyes closed. "That tired me out more than I thought it would." I heard him scoot the guest chair out of the corner, and opened my eyes to see him sitting in it, facing me. "Yes, I took it off. It was in the drawer over there." I pointed to the bedside table, where the drawer hung open and empty.

"Why?"

I sighed. Then I told him what had really happened: that the thunderbird spirit had called Sandy Mishepeshu and set him on fire. "I'd guess the glow on my back was the turtle's way of protecting me," I said. "My doctor said he was surprised that my injuries hadn't been more severe."

Rick nodded. "So you took off the necklace because you didn't trust the bird effigy."

"It went rogue on me!" I said. "*No*, I don't trust it. I didn't have any use for Sandy, but I sure didn't ask it to set him on fire!"

"Or set the house on fire," he said. "Or kill your mom."

My lower lip began to tremble. "God, Rick. I don't know what I'm going to do." I tried to blink back the tears, but they fell anyway. "What am I gonna do?"

He took my hand and patted it. "We'll figure it out."

I nodded and withdrew my hand.

"I'm so very sorry about your mom. She was a good woman."

"She was." I wiped my eyes with the edge of the bedsheet. "She put up with a lot."

He nodded. "So when are they letting you out of this joint?"

"Tomorrow, or so I hear. Mom's memorial service is Monday." I snorted a laugh. "Great start to the week, huh? But I was grateful that the funeral home agreed to wait 'til I got out of here."

"That was kind of them," he agreed. "Uh, when is Sandy's service?"

"It was yesterday. In Indy." I didn't have to add that I wasn't sorry to have missed it. I was fiercely grateful that both he and Diane were out of my life, and I felt no remorse for it.

"Do you have a place to go?"

I laughed. "Yeah. The Red Cross got me a sweet little room in a no-tell motel."

He cleared his throat. "You know you have a place to stay. If you want it." I looked up at him in alarm. "No strings," he added hastily.

"Well, thanks. I appreciate the offer." I breathed in. "Let me think about it. For now, I think I need some privacy."

"Of course. Makes perfect sense." He rose and went to the door. "I'll field any more calls from the police. If they contact you, tell them to call me."

"Will do."

"And call me when you're released. I'll come and pick you up. Where's your car?"

I blinked. "Still parked in front of Mom's house, I guess."

So when I was released, late the next day, Rick picked me up. On my way out, the nurse handed me my discharge paperwork – including a prescription for a painkiller. I regarded it for a moment. "Is this an opioid?" I asked her.

She glanced at it. "Yes. Why?"

I handed it back to her. "Because they killed my sister-in-law," I said. "Thanks, but no."

The nurse looked from me to Rick. "She's not kidding," he said. She shrugged and stuck it in her pocket. I hoped she would shred it later.

Then Rick drove me to Mom's to pick up my car.

I thought I knew what to expect, but when I saw the hulking remnants of my childhood home, I still felt punched in the gut. Mom's and Sandy's vehicles were still parked in the driveway, their front ends looking like they'd been firebombed.

"Lucky those cars didn't go up with the house," Rick said.

"Yeah," I said vaguely, and got out.

He waited at the curb while I picked my way into the charred wreckage. The concrete porch steps led nowhere now; I walked straight through what had been the living room wall and made my way gingerly to where my room would have been, dodging the yellow tape that still marked where Mom's and Sandy's bodies had been found.

Of all the things I had moved into my mother's place, there was only one thing that I hoped had survived the fire: the shoebox that held my children's mementoes. But it was gone. It had only been cardboard, and it went up in flames with everything else.

"Maggie?" Rick called. I realized I'd been standing in the same spot for quite a while.

"Yeah," I responded, and stepped over what was left of the wall and into the backyard. Then I circled around where the kitchen and utility room had been, and rejoined him at the curb. "There's nothing left," I said, and let him hold me.

"I seen what you did," someone send over Rick's shoulder.

We turned as one, and I peered at the newcomer. "Eddie?"

Ed Byrum looked terrible: sunken eyes, hollow cheeks. He'd grown up on our street and had occasionally palled around with Sandy when we were kids. He didn't go to high school with us, though. Rumor had it that he'd been sent to reform school for grand theft auto.

"I seen what you did, Maggie," he repeated. "You torched your own brother and burned your own house down. I seen it!"

"You're the one who called the fire department, aren't you?" I said.

"Yeah, and I told 'em what you did!" he said. "Why ain't you in jail?"

"Maybe because I didn't torch my own brother and burn my own house down," I said.

"Eddie," Rick said, "do the cops know you're dealing?" With that, I realized why the guy looked so awful – he had the same gaunt, sickly look about him that Sandy had had.

"You just shut your damn mouth!" he yelled. "They can't pin anything on me!"

"Let's go," I said to Rick. "Nice talking to you, Eddie."

"You don't even care what you done, do you?" he yelled. "I was gonna be set for life!"

Rick paused as he was about to open the driver's side door of my car. "What do you mean by that?"

He stepped up to me and growled in my face, "Don't tell me you didn't know anything about it, Miss High and Mighty. Sandy had it all figured out. He was gonna move his mom into a rest home and give me the house. But *you* had to fuck it up."

I took a step back. "Give *you* the house?"

"To pay off his drug debts," said Rick, sounding tired. "Get lost, Eddie, before I call the cops on you."

Eddie looked back and forth at us, as it dawned on him what he had just copped to. "It was his idea," he said.

"I'm sure it was," said Rick. "Scram."

"Jesus. You're a lawyer, ain't you?" Eddie said, backpedaling. "Go ahead and call the cops!" he yelled over his shoulder as he beat a retreat. "You can't pin anything on me!"

Chapter 16

Rick followed me to the motel. It was not a seduction attempt at all — he was businesslike about it. I wasn't sure how I felt about that.

I wasn't sure how I felt about anything any more.

But I was grateful for his presence. I'd called the place a no-tell motel as a joke, but it turned out I wasn't far off the mark. My car was the newest one parked in the lot, other than Rick's. And it was clear many of the guests were actually long-term residents. I saw laundry festooned on the curtain rods inside some units, and a couple of places had barbeque kettles and folding chairs on the sidewalk that ran along the front of the building. Maybe they were all nice people, but I didn't expect to stay long enough to find out.

"Sorry for your troubles," the clerk in the office said when I collected my key.

"Thanks. How much do I owe you?" I dug in my purse for my wallet.

"Oh, you don't have to pay. The room is paid up through the end of the week." She handed over the key card with a second-floor room number written in marker on the paper sleeve. "Wi-fi is extra, though."

I thought of my tablet, which I'd decided against taking to work with me the day of the fire. "Thanks, but I won't need it."

"Okay, well, enjoy your stay." Suddenly embarrassed, she scuttled away. I couldn't blame her. There wasn't much that was going to be enjoyable about the next week.

Rick was waiting on the sidewalk when I emerged. "I'll walk you up," he said.

"You don't need to."

"Damn it, Maggie, let me do this for you," he said, exasperated.

I blinked. "Well, okay." And we walked side by side up the stairs to the second floor.

"You don't have to go through this by yourself," he said. "There are people who would love to help you. All you have to do is ask."

"I'd like for you to help me get the stuff out of your trunk," I said with a teasing smile. "But I want to see the state of the room first."

It wasn't terrible. The place was clean; the linens were worn, but in good repair. There was a mini-fridge, atop of which was a miniature microwave and the ubiquitous motel coffee maker. The TV worked and so did the heater. "Home, sweet home," I said, dropping my purse on top of the microwave. "Let's go get my new stuff."

There wasn't much: A trash bag full of clothes in my size, more or less, and a box of castoff kitchen items. The latter included a crockpot that the motel probably wouldn't allow me to use. Then again, they allowed grills. Or maybe they didn't.

My stomach rumbled, reminding me it was past suppertime. "I heard that," Rick said, and we both laughed. "Want to grab a bite?"

"Nah," I said. "Thanks, though. I think I need to be alone tonight."

"Okay. Can't fault a guy for trying."

"I don't. Not at all." I smiled warmly at him.

"Well. I'll see you at the service tomorrow, then," he said.

"Nine o'clock," I said. "Don't be late." I walked him to the door and said, "Seriously, Rick, thanks for everything. I couldn't have gotten this far without you. You've been a rock."

He nodded, kissed my cheek, and let himself out.

When I was alone at last, I let the tears flow.

I'd been holding them back for so long that they came out in giant, gulping, inelegant sobs. I'd lost everything – literally. The only things that had survived the conflagration had been with me: my shoes, my purse, my car. The back of my puffy winter jacket had melted and fused with my polyester uniform top; if I hadn't been wearing a cotton turtleneck underneath it all, my back would have been burned much worse. My phone, which had been in my pants pocket, had survived. My necklace, which had been around my neck, had also survived. And that was it. All I owned in the world was reduced to a set of aging wheels, a purse full of old receipts, a tube of lip balm, and a pair of ugly shoes.

And the necklace.

I pulled it out of my purse and hung it on one corner of the back of the desk chair. I was done with wearing it. I wasn't even sure I wanted to carry it around with me anymore; maybe I'd keep it in the fridge.

No.

I froze. It was the voice from my dream. The same voice that had called my brother Mishepeshu before setting him afire.

Do not abandon us. A different voice. Kinder.

The necklace swayed slightly to and fro, although there was no breeze in the room.

I sank slowly onto the edge of the mattress, keeping my eyes on the necklace the whole time. I wasn't scared, exactly, but I was cautious. No, nervous. Definitely nervous. "Why should I keep you around?" I said aloud. "You killed my brother and my mother. All my stuff is gone. The house I grew up in is gone."

Yes. The thunderbird again.

"Why?" I repeated.

It was necessary.

I got up and stalked toward the bathroom. Then I turned and stalked back, hands on hips. "I need a better answer than that," I said.

I half expected silence, or something to the effect that I should be happy to have received any answer at all. Instead, the bird said, *The rot had to be excised. You were not ready to do it yourself.*

"Rot?" I cried. "What does *that* mean?"

Sit, Nokomtha, the kinder voice said, and now I recognized it, too. This was the voice that had first whispered that name to me as my granddaughter, Royce, was trying to decide what to call me. It meant "grandmother" in Shawnee.

The turtle hadn't steered me wrong yet, so I sat on the edge of the bed again. As soon as my butt hit the mattress, I was…

…in the woods near the stream where I'd first encountered Mishepeshu stalking my mother the doe. Neither Mom nor Mishepeshu/Sandy were there now; instead, a large turtle sat on the bank of the stream. Her shell was at least five feet in diameter and was etched with designs I recognized as both the path of earth's renewal and the path of my own life.

Above the turtle, perched on a branch, was the flaming bird.

Who was I in this dreamscape? I glanced down at my hands. They looked normal – human-shaped and clothed in human flesh.

I drew a relieved breath and said, "Why have you brought me here?"

"We need to talk of important matters," said the turtle, "and it's more easily done here than in mindspeak."

"We are less likely to be interrupted here," the bird said. It settled itself on the branch, sending a cascade of sparks into the water.

"All right, then," I said. "Answer my questions. What do you mean by rot? And why was it necessary to kill my…"

"I told you she wouldn't understand," the bird said scornfully.

"But she can," said the turtle in an even tone. "She must."

I was beginning to lose patience. "Explain it to me, then. In tiny words, if that's all you've got."

"She's sneering," the bird said. "I told you…"

"Hush," the turtle said to us both. Then she focused on me. "Nokomtha, we know this has been difficult for you. Please understand that we would have been more gentle with you if we had had more time."

More time? "Is this about Granny?" I asked.

"In part."

Now I was concerned. "How is she?" I wished I had some way to contact Zed. Maybe if I called all the hospitals in Louisville – but I didn't even know Granny's real name…

"You will know soon enough. Attend!" the bird said, and sent another shower of sparks into the stream. "Did Turtle not say time was growing short?"

"All right. I'm sorry. I'll be more patient."

The bird snorted. "Go on, then, Turtle, if you can."

"*I can, and I will,*" *Turtle said equably.* "*Nokomtha, our friend Thunderbird possesses a difficult temper.*"

"*I noticed that.*"

"*But she is right in saying there was rot in your family.*"

"*But I repudiated my brother. I heard the door shut.*"

"*He was not the only one.*"

I frowned. "*You can't possibly mean my mother.*"

"*Nokomtha,*" *said Turtle.* "*What was the last thing your mother said to you about your brother?*"

I thought back to the last conversation we'd had about him. "*She said the same thing she always does. Did.*" *I paused for a moment as her death hit me again. Then I continued,* "*She told me I had to get along with him, because once she died, he would be all I had left.*"

"*Was that true?*"

"*Not now, it's not,*" *I said acidly. When Turtle didn't react, I dialed it back.* "*Of course not. I have my own children. And I have friends. Abby and Sallie. And Rick. And my boss at the grocery store. And Granny and Zed.*" *I paused.* "*And you two, I guess.*"

Turtle dipped her head. "*So why would your mother have said that to you? She knew your brother had abused you as a child. And he was not kind to her, either, as you know.*"

"*She always blamed Diane for the way Sandy treated her,*" *I said slowly.* "*But it went much farther back.*" *A memory came to me suddenly, from when Sandy was in high school and I was in junior high. Mom had just forbidden him from doing something he wanted to do — go out drinking, maybe, or take the car and stay out late — and he backhanded her across the mouth. Mom burst into tears and ran to her bedroom. Sandy threatened me with the same treatment he'd just given Mom if I breathed a word of it to Dad. Then he left. And as far as I knew, Dad never found out. Regardless, Sandy was never punished.*

Mom had accused me of playing the victim when it came to Sandy. But I never had. I just wanted him to be held accountable for his transgressions. Mom had avoided confronting him about his behavior by setting me up as an example of the perfect child – but that had backfired on all three of us.

"She wanted everybody to get along," I said. "By any means necessary."

"And by doing that, she compounded the damage done to you," Turtle said.

"I never felt understood," I said. "I never felt that my pain was acknowledged."

"It wasn't," Turtle said. "It was swept under the rug."

"Why?" I said. "Why would she treat me that way? She loved me."

"Was her family perfect?" Thunderbird asked.

"Yeah, it…well." I paused. "Come to think of it, probably not. My grandfather drank a lot." I remembered visits to the family farm. Grandpa Denison would invite Dad and Uncle Freddy, Aunt Helen's husband, to have a drink. Pretty soon Grandpa would have a snootful and would turn loud and mean. We left for home early pretty often. "But Mom never said a bad word about Grandpa. I suppose Grandma trained the kids to act as if everything was fine." A terrible thought struck me. "Oh, God."

"Yes?" Turtle asked.

I said quietly, "I did the same thing. I covered for Gene. All those years, I pretended everything was fine." I looked at Turtle and Thunderbird. "That's the rot, isn't it?"

"Yes," Turtle said. "Not the sickness. Every family has its problems, some terrible and some not so bad. But sickness can't be healed if no one will acknowledge its existence."

"In time," Thunderbird said, "you would have come to this realization on your own. But events were moving too quickly. Your brother was sinking too fast, and events in the wider world are proceeding faster than we had anticipated. I had to act." She paused. "I am sorry to have caused you this pain, Nokomtha."

The bird sounded sincere, but I wasn't ready to be mollified just yet. "Thanks," I said. "But there's more to it. The police think I'm the one who caused the fire."

"You would be imprisoned?" Turtle asked in dismay.

"If I'm arrested, tried, and found guilty, yes. And all that will take time. Months, if not years."

"We cannot afford another delay," Turtle said.

"I will fix this," said Thunderbird, and disappeared, shedding a few fiery feathers in her wake. They drifted down to the stream, where they sizzled and went out.

Turtle swung her head around to me. "I too am sorry, Nokomtha. I wish this could have been done another way."

"So do I," I said, "but what's done is done. Still, thank you. It might have taken me years to put two and two together." I sighed. "This has been quite the growth experience. First Gene's side of the family, and our kids, and now this. Is there more to come?"

"Not much more," Turtle said, and took us back.

I was once again seated on the edge of the mattress in my well-worn motel room. My necklace still hung, no longer moving, on the back of the straight-backed chair.

My cheeks were still wet with tears; I wiped them on the sleeve of my shirt. More tears would come, I knew. But for now, I sat quietly and thought through what Turtle and Thunderbird had told me.

I had sometimes wondered, in the years since our divorce, why I'd never turned Gene in. It had never occurred to me that the impetus to keep the family together at all costs had come from behavior I'd witnessed at home.

If Mom had acknowledged Sandy's abuse, what would have happened? Today's parents would take a troubled kid to a therapist. Ideally, I mean – some would still stick their heads in the sand and believe their little darlings were incapable of doing any wrong. But in general, there would be a consultation with the pediatrician and then a visit or three with a counselor. Or maybe the kid would be sent to a special school.

But in the sixties? Psychologists were popularly known as headshrinkers, and people of my parents' socioeconomic class didn't believe anybody needed one. Mental problems were treated as behavioral issues. Kids who acted out got a paddling. Kids who complained about their siblings were told to shut up.

Maybe Mom didn't want Dad to hit Sandy. Maybe she didn't want Dad to know his family was less than perfect. Or maybe she thought Sandy's behavior – and mine – would reflect poorly on her as a mother.

In my own case, Ruth already thought I was a lousy mother, so of *course* I wanted to preserve the illusion of the perfect family.

I couldn't find it in my heart to fault my mother. She was who she was. Yes, she refused to acknowledge my pain. But she did the best she could, given her own upbringing and the era she lived in. And if I couldn't fault *her*, how could I beat myself up for doing the same thing she did?

When I came to that realization, I felt something shift in my head. It was almost a physical sensation – as if my old thought pattern had been jarred loose from its track and shoved into a new one. The new groove was a little wobbly, but it felt right.

I gathered up my necklace almost reverently and put it on. Then I picked up my purse and skipped down to my car to get dinner. I was still grieving, and I had a big job ahead of me, but I felt oddly free – freer than I could ever remember feeling. My oldest pain and suffering had been brought out into the light and acknowledged, and I knew now that I'd been right all along: you can't *play the victim* if you really have been victimized.

Chapter 17

I made sure to arrive at the funeral home early, but I wasn't the first person there. Rick was speaking to the assistant funeral director at the front of the room. I hung my coat on the rack at the back of the room and approached the casket.

It was closed, of course. Sprays of flowers, paid for by Mom's estate, stood at the head and foot. I'd picked pink and purple gladiolus because they were her favorite; I remembered them standing like sentinels along the front of the house every summer. I wondered whether they would come up this year, without the house behind them for support. I supposed they would.

I wondered whether I would still be here in Lawrenceburg to see them. I suspected not.

I placed my hand on Mom's casket and whispered, "I'm so sorry. I wish I could have saved you. I wish I could have saved us both." I dropped my head and folded my hands as if in prayer, though I was not praying. Then I went on, still in a whisper, "I don't fault you for what you did. I know you did what you thought was right, just as I did with my own kids. We are all human and we all make mistakes. All any of us can do is our best."

I touched the coffin again. "I love you, Mom." Then I walked over to where Rick waited for me.

I gave him a hug and shook hands with the funeral director. We went over the service briefly: the current preacher for the Methodist church we'd attended when I was little had agreed to preside, and so there would be a homily and a hymn or two. I insisted on saying a few words myself; Rick looked at me curiously, and the funeral home guy seemed doubtful but agreed. It didn't matter to me whether he said it was okay or not – I intended to do it anyway.

Not long after that, people began arriving. First in the door was Ron, my boss at the grocery store. "This is such a horrible thing. I can't believe you're upright. How are you feeling? How are your injuries healing?"

"I'm well, thanks," I said. "A twinge now and then, but that's all."

He seemed relieved. "Well, however long you need to take off," he said, "do it. Don't worry about your job. I'll hold it open for you."

"Thank you," I said. "I can't tell you how much I appreciate it. But how will you square it with corporate?"

He grinned. "I just won't tell them."

More of my co-workers came, including Marty, my favorite bagger. He shook hands shyly and mumbled his condolences, then sat as far from the action as possible while still being in the same room.

And then my family walked in: Bea and John and the little ones, Royce and Ryker; Abby and Sallie, without the baby; Abby's older sister Debbie, of all people, escorted by her firstborn, Lee; and – the biggest surprise of all – Ruth, using a cane, and Riley riding shotgun.

"Nokomtha!" Royce cried, and ran to me.

I scooped her up, laughing and crying at the same time. "I am so glad to see you," I said, nuzzling her hair. By that time, her mother and father had reached me, and hugs were exchanged all around.

Even Ryker forgot to be shy and reached out for me. "Noko," he said, resting his head briefly in the crook of my neck. I kissed him and handed him back to his father so I could greet everyone else.

"How are you doing, Mom?" Bea asked.

"Fine. We'll talk later," I said, and moved on to give Riley a hug. "I didn't expect to see you here, but I'm glad you came," I said.

"I didn't expect to be here, either," she said, flipping her long hair back over one shoulder. "But Ruth wanted to come, and God knows Gene wouldn't bring her."

"And thank goodness for that," I said. "Hello, Ruth. Glad to see you."

"I bet you never thought you'd say *that*, did you?" she said, and cackled. "I just couldn't let you go through this alone. Your mother gone, and the house, too." She shook her head. Then she got a crafty look in her eye. "At least you still have my place."

"Don't you start that with me," I said, shaking a finger at her. "Not today." I turned to give Debbie a hug. "Thank you for coming. Hello, Lee." I shook hands with him and moved down the line to Abby and Sallie. "I'm glad to see you guys again so soon, but where's Bernice?"

"Emily's taking care of her," Abby said. "We didn't want to put her on an airplane again so soon, and Em had time, now that she's on winter break."

"Em didn't come, then?" I asked, trying to swallow my disappointment.

"No," said Bea, "and neither did Tim. He's still in Mexico City with Ana."

"Well," I said brightly, "I'm glad you all could make it. I'm grateful for the support."

"Attending funerals is about all I do these days," said Ruth. "I'm getting pretty good at it." She noticed a man in clerical garb making his way to the front of the room. "Say, what kind of rabbi is that?"

"The Methodist kind," I said tartly. "Excuse me, everyone. I need to have a word with him before we start."

The service was lovely. The preacher, who had only met my mother once, did a credible job with the notes I'd given him. I made sure he mentioned my brother, but nixed the idea to glorify both Mom and Sandy in his remarks. "He meant to kill her," I stressed. "He meant to kill both of us. I'm not sorry he's gone."

"Got it," he said – and he did. During the service, he only mentioned Sandy's name once. I was able to tolerate that.

When it was my turn to speak, I stepped to the podium and said, "My mother, Shirley Denison Muir, was a survivor. She was one of five children, three boys and two girls. One of her brothers died in infancy, and the other two were killed in World War II. She and her sister, my aunt Helen, were the only children who survived into adulthood. Then her parents died, and Aunt Helen and Uncle Freddy took over the farm for good – they'd already been running it for some time. But then they both died, too, when I was in my teens. After that, it was just my mother, my father, my brother Sandy, and me. That was our whole family.

"Mom survived the death of my father, George Muir. And she thrived for a long time. When her memory started to fail not long ago, I moved in with her. She had survived so many things that even though she was eighty-eight, I was pretty sure she would outlive us all. Even me." Polite laughter.

"Of course, Mom couldn't survive forever. None of us can. Now I'm the survivor." I paused. "I will always remember my mother for her lemon chiffon pies and the gladiolus that bloomed at our house every summer. I'll remember the green dress she went all the way to Cincinnati for, because she couldn't find anything that suited her here in Lawrenceburg. She got her money's worth out of that dress. She wore it to my high school graduation and Sandy's wedding, and my wedding, too." More polite laughter. "But mostly I'll remember the love she had for all of us. And I will always remember that no matter her failings – and she had them, as we all do – she always did the best she could with what she had."

"That was beautiful," Bea whispered as I resumed my seat.

"Thanks. You know it was in code, right?" I whispered back.

"Of course," she said. "But it was still beautiful."

We rented a meeting room at a hotel near the funeral home for the post-service meal. The grocery store sent over a bunch of platters – cold cuts, veggies, fruit trays and desserts.

At last, I had time to introduce Rick to everyone. He seemed a little overwhelmed, but I understood – it was a lot of people to keep straight. "I'm sure I'll forget everyone's name," he said more than once.

"Next time we'll wear name tags to make it easier on you," said Ruth.

Rick laughed and said, "You, I'll remember."

Eventually, everyone left but the immediate family and Rick. "Okay, Mom – spill it," Bea said when it was just us. "How are you doing, how's your back, where are you gonna live now, and all that stuff."

"My back is fine," I said. "The burns weren't that bad, and the soreness is mostly gone. As for how I'm doing…" I paused. "I'm fine right now. I'm making peace with everything that happened. And I've realized that your grandmother wasn't a saint. She could have put a stop to what Uncle Sandy did to me, but she wanted to pretend that everything was fine. So when your father…" I let the sentence hang.

"You pretended everything was fine," Bea finished. "Because that's what you learned as a kid. Oh, Mom, I'm so sorry I ever judged you."

"It's okay," I said. "I deserved it at the time. I'm glad we're clearing the air now."

Ruth spoke up. "Don't judge your mother too harshly. Shirley and I grew up in the same era, you know, and people didn't talk about this kind of stuff back then. You kept your family business to yourself." She sniffed. "Nowadays, everybody's gotta air their dirty laundry."

"Yeah, we do, Ma," Debbie said. "It's healthier that way, just like Bea and Maggie said."

Abby chimed in – to agree with her sister, no doubt – but I barely heard her. For I had spied two more people coming in the door: Zed and Granny.

"Excuse me," I said, and rose in a hurry to greet them. I almost didn't recognize them. Granny was moving, but slowly, pushing a walker and wincing with every step. She had set aside her usual pastel-colored tracksuit for a pair of black slacks and a subdued blouse. Zed had ditched the tie-dye-and-bandanna look for dark slacks and a polo shirt.

"Sorry we're late," Zed said as I reached them. "We meant to be here for the funeral service, but we got held up."

"Don't worry about it. I'm glad you came at all," I said, smiling. "I've been so worried about you both. Come on – I want you to meet my family."

"We can't stay," said Granny. "We've lost too much time as it is."

I stopped in mid-stride and turned back to them. "People keep telling me that time is growing short," I said. "But no one has told me why."

Zed glanced at Granny. "Go on," he said. "Tell her."

"Dear Margie," she said.

"Maggie," Zed and I said together.

"Maggie," she said. "Right. Look. While I was in the hospital with this dad-blamed hip, the doctors found something else."

"Cancer," Zed said.

"Oh, no," I said. "How bad is it? I mean..."

"Oh, don't worry," she said. "I'm not gonna die any time soon. But like your former mother-in-law over there, I'm gonna need surgery, and then probably chemo or something." She touched her white bun absently. "I'm not looking forward to losing my hair. But that's not the point." She dropped her arm. "The point is that this is gonna sideline me for several months."

"So..."

"We need to have you step up," Zed said. "Take on some of Granny's work, so she doesn't fall behind."

"I know it's lousy timing," Granny said. "With you having just lost your mother and all. And I know you're settled in here."

I looked at the meeting room where my family clustered around a table, all of them from out of town. "Actually," I said, "this would be a pretty good time for me to go. There's not much of anything to hold me here in Lawrenceburg now that Mom's gone."

"What about him?" Zed asked, pointing at Rick, sitting in the midst of all those people I loved. He sure looked to me like he fit in. But I knew that wasn't what counted.

I turned back to Zed and Granny. "If it's meant to be, he'll still be here when I get back."

They exchanged a dubious look. Then Zed shrugged. "Well, okay. If you say so."

"Look," I said. "How do I start? How will I know where to go?"

"Oh, I'm not having this done right away," Granny said. "No, I have to finish the physical therapy for my hip. Then they'll cut me open and all the rest."

"Don't talk like that," Zed said.

Granny hooked a thumb at him. "He hates sickness."

"I do," he said.

"Faints at the sight of blood."

He looked hard at her. "I do not!"

She grinned. "Anyhow, you have a couple of months before you need to take over from me. You could stay here and keep working at the grocery store, and keep dating Mr. I'm Not Sure I'm Ready over there." She nodded at Rick with a wicked smile. "Or you could do something else. Something you've always wanted to do that you've never been able to."

"Travel," I said instantly. "Not like you and Zed do, but maybe in an RV. You know, see the country. I've never been anywhere but here, Indianapolis, and Rockville." A sudden desire to see my daughter Emily seized me. "And I want to see my kids. Bea's here today, but I haven't seen Emily in ages. And Tim's stuck in Mexico with his girlfriend. I need to see them. Talk face-to-face with them."

Smiles dawned on their faces. "It's working," Zed said. "That's how you know."

"What?"

"What you were just asking. How to know where to go? That's how you know," he said.

"That overwhelming urge you just felt," Granny said.

"Really? Huh." I considered that. "It's good to know what to look out for."

"Good. I'm glad that's settled. Lovely to see you," Granny said, and began inching her walker around to leave.

"Oh, no!" I said, dismayed. "Can't you stay for a little while?"

"Sorry," Zed said. "She's the boss. We'll have time to meet everybody later. Won't we, Granny?"

She looked over her shoulder, head nodding slightly, as she perused the group. "Yes, indeed, we will. And I'm looking forward to it." She patted my arm. "Goodbye, Maggie."

"You remembered my name," I said. "You know, with Mom gone, you're the only one who ever calls me Margie."

"I wonder why that is," she said mysteriously. And with a wave, she and Zed disappeared through the doorway.

I waved back, and then rejoined the group at the table. "Maggie, where's the bathroom?" Ruth asked as I sat down.

"I'm not sure," I said. "Down the hall toward the lobby, I think."

"You're not sure? Weren't you just there?"

"No, I was talking to the people by the door." I gestured toward the entrance. "The old lady with the walker and the guy with the ponytail." I looked around the table of mystified faces. "You guys didn't see them?"

"No," said Rick.

"I did!" Royce cried.

"Royce," Bea said. "Maybe it was a different old lady you saw."

"Nooo, it was her," my granddaughter insisted. "She was dressed all in pink the other time. And she said she knew Nokomtha."

Bea looked at her husband, who shrugged.

"We can find the bathroom together, Ruth," Riley said. She had to pass behind me to get to Ruth; on the way, she bent over and whispered in my ear, "I saw them, too."

"Thanks for letting me know I'm not crazy," I said with a grin.

"No problem," she said, and went on her way.

I turned then to Rick. "So how long do you think it will take to settle Mom's estate?"

He shrugged. "A month, maybe. Her finances were very simple – the biggest delay will be the insurance payment for the house. Why?"

"I'm thinking I'd like to take some time off and travel," I said. "Maybe get an RV. What do you think?"

He stared at me. "Have we had this conversation?"

"I don't think so. Why?"

"Because I've been thinking of doing that for years."

I grinned. "Want to come with me?"

He opened his mouth. Closed it. Pondered for a moment. "Let me think about it," he said at last.

"Take all the time you need," I said, even though I knew I wouldn't wait too long. I needed to get back on my path without further delay.

Beneath my blouse, against my skin, my turtle and bird warmed in agreement.

Author's Note

This was a difficult book for me to write, as some of the themes hit close to home.

Not the drug abuse – and I'm grateful for that. Opioids are now the major cause of accidental death in the United States. The National Institute on Drug Abuse estimates that in 2015, two million Americans abused these prescription pain medicines – oxycodone (OxyContin is one brand name), hydrocodone, codeine, morphine, fentanyl, and other drugs – and another 591,000 abused heroin. More than 33,000 Americans died that year by overdosing on opioid medications. And the death toll is rising; deaths due to opioids were higher in the first nine months of 2016 than in the same period the previous year. A presidential commission recently reported the death toll is so bad now, in 2017, it's as if the nation were experiencing "September 11th every three weeks."

Part of the jump in the fatality rate is attributable to dealers who are more frequently cutting heroin with fentanyl – a powerful animal tranquilizer on which humans can overdose simply by touching it with their bare hands.

Earlier this month, the Trump administration declared the opioid crisis a national emergency. That should help with things like getting naloxone into the hands of first responders – but naloxone is not a universal antidote, and in some cases it can take multiple doses to revive someone who has OD'd.

Figures on verbal and emotional abuse are not as concrete. But the National Coalition Against Domestic Violence says nearly half of all people – women *and* men – have experienced at least one episode of psychologically aggressive behavior by a partner. And 95 percent of physically abusive men also use psychological abuse tactics on their victims. Seventy percent of women who have experienced psychological abuse show symptoms of depression and/or post-traumatic stress disorder, also known as PTSD. Abusers don't have to be adults; I was verbally abused all through my growing-up years, and I know first-hand how destructive it can be.

If you or someone you know is in an abusive situation – physical, psychological, or both – please visit the NCADV's website at http://ncadv.org, or call the National Domestic Violence Hotline at 1-800-799-SAFE.

On to less fraught topics.

Thanks, as always, to my editors, Susan Strayer and Kat Milyko – in particular for their careful editing when I couldn't bring myself to read about Maggie's family issues one more time.

If you enjoyed this book – or not – I'd love it if you would go back where you purchased it and post a review. Reviews are a key way that readers find good books, and I treasure each and every review that my books receive.

You're also warmly invited to join my Woo-Woo Team. We meet on Facebook at https://www.facebook.com/groups/WooWooTeam/. You have to ask to join, but so far I've let everybody in, so your odds of acceptance are spectacular. I'd love to see you there.

One more thing: To get the first word on all of my new releases, please go to http://eepurl.com/xxw9d to sign up for my spam-free newsletter. It's your guaranteed way to find out what's coming up, and I only darken your inbox with them three or four times a year.

Now that *Maggie on the Cusp* is out of my head and in your hands, dear reader, I'm confident I'll be able to finish the trilogy this fall. Look for *Maggie at Moonrise* in late November.

Lynne Cantwell
August 2017

About the Author

Lynne Cantwell writes mostly urban fantasy and paranormal romance, with a dash of magic realism when she's feeling more serious. She is also a contributing author for Indies Unlimited. In a previous life, she was a broadcast journalist who worked at Mutual/NBC Radio News, CNN, and a bunch of other places you have probably never heard of. She has a master's degree in fiction writing from Johns Hopkins University. Currently, she lives near Washington, D.C.

Discover other titles by Lynne Cantwell:

The Pipe Woman Chronicles Universe
Seized: Book One of the Pipe Woman Chronicles
Fissured: Book Two of the Pipe Woman Chronicles
Tapped: Book Three of the Pipe Woman Chronicles
Gravid: Book Four of the Pipe Woman Chronicles
Annealed: Book Five of the Pipe Woman Chronicles
The Pipe Woman Chronicles Omnibus

Where Were You When: A Land, Sea, Sky Anthology
Crosswind: Land, Sea, Sky Book 1
Undertow: Land, Sea, Sky Book 2
Scorched Earth: Land, Sea, Sky Book 3
The Land Sea Sky Trilogy

Dragon's Web: Book One of the Pipe Woman's Legacy
Firebird's Snare: Book Two of the Pipe Woman's Legacy
Spider's Lifeline: Book Three of the Pipe Woman's Legacy

Turtle's Weir: Book Four of the Pipe Woman's Legacy

A Billion Gods and Goddesses: The Mythology Behind *The Pipe Woman Chronicles*

The Transcendence Trilogy
Maggie in the Dark: Transcendence Book 1
Maggie on the Cusp: Transcendence Book 2
Maggie at Moonrise: Transcendence Book 3 (coming fall 2017)

Stand-Alone Novels
SwanSong
The Maidens' War
Seasons of the Fool

Short Story Collections
Back Home Again: The Five59 Stories, plus a few

Contributor
Indies Unlimited 2012 Flash Fiction Anthology
Indies Unlimited 2013 Flash Fiction Anthology
Indies Unlimited 2014 Flash Fiction Anthology
Indies Unlimited Tutorials and Tools for Prospering in a Digital World
Indies Unlimited Tutorials and Tools for Prospering in a Digital World,
Vol. II
13 Bites
Summer Dreams
Boo!: Volume 2
Winter Tales
Plan 559 from Outer Space
Other Realms

13 Bites Vol. III
I Heard It on the Radio
Plan 559 from Outer Space Mk. II
Other Realms Volume II
13 Bites Vol. IV
Plan 559 from Outer Space Mk. III
Free for All: A Writers' Anthology

Find Lynne on Teh Intarwebz:

Facebook: http://www.facebook.com/pages/Lynne-Cantwell
Twitter: http://twitter.com/lynnecantwell
Google Plus: http://plus.google.com/+LynneCantwell
Goodreads:
http://www.goodreads.com/author/show/696603.Lynne_Cantwell
Blog: http://www.hearth-myth.com

www.ingramcontent.com/pod-product-compliance
Lightning Source LLC
Chambersburg PA
CBHW071916220626
47052CB00002B/372